PRESIDENT'S AGENT

PRESIDENT'S AGENT

JOSEPH HILTON

ISBN-13: 978-1-970848-02-1

Published by
Cutting Edge Books
PO Box 8212
Calabasas, CA 91372
www.cuttingedgebooks.com

PROLOGUE

MANUEL ORTEGA, chauffeur of long standing for the United States Embassy in Colima, San Barrios, slammed his foot down hard on the brake pedal as the car headlights picked out the dark hulks blocking the curving road ahead. He blared the horn. Slowly one of the shapeless masses moved, took form, became a steer lumbering lethargically towards the side of the road.

Manuel swore without rancor. Sooner or later the horn and glaring headlights would clear the road of the animals bedded stubbornly down for the night on the hard pavement that still held pleasant warmth from the day's hot sun. But tonight even a minor delay was unfortunate. For he had shaved the time of his scheduled pick-up of Señor Drake, whom he was to drive to the airport in Punta Helvos, a little too close. Thanks to Carmelita.

No, he decided reasonably, the fault had been equally his. He should have contented himself with eating a supper in the kitchen of the Embassy. Instead he had asked for and received permission to drive out to his modest home in Magdalena, some 15 kilometers distance, to enjoy *cena* with his young wife. He should have known what would happen. It was what, most delightfully, always happened.

Still playing automatically on the horn, waiting for the road to clear, Manuel sighed longingly as he thought of Carmelita's warm brown body and the tightening embrace of her thighs when she felt his manhood within her. A woman who was all woman—and always eager to prove it! *Hijo,* but he was a lucky man.

He grinned at himself as he felt remembered passion stir in his loins. He should be thinking of other things—most particularly of el señor Drake, a man who was extremely precise about appointments being kept on the dot. Manuel sighed again and lit a cigarette. Then he looked up as the rear-view mirror reflected the headlights of an on coming car. *Bueno,* let someone else clear the road of stubbornly slumbering beasts.

His smile faded suddenly and was replaced by a faint frown. The car behind him was coming on too fast, almost as though it were in pursuit. Yet it carried no red light on its top to indicate that it belonged to the *departmento de transito.* Not that that mattered; diplomatic plates on his car made Manuel pridefully secure from the mordida-hungry police.

Yet planned purpose, rather than simple reckless driving, suggested the manner in which the big, dusty sedan now swerved left until screeching brakes and the whine of protesting tires halted it abreast of Manuel's car. And the same planned purpose in the swinging open of the rear door even before the sedan had slithered to a full stop.

The wary instinct of the Indio, bred through centuries of oppression, warned Manuel. Stomach muscles suddenly tight, he lunged for the gun secreted in the glove compartment.

A matter of a split second to fling himself sideways across the seat and press the button that flipped open the compartment door. He reached in—and his grasping fingers closed on a wedged-in package wrapped in paper. Food—most probably some tacos and a dulce—that Carmelita had lovingly prepared as a surprise. A tender, wifely gesture that now blocked the one small fighting chance Manuel might have had.

As he frantically clawed past the package the car door was wrenched violently open. Manuel half turned his head—and froze motionless. And not alone because of the .45 leveled at his belly—it was the appearance of the creature holding the ugly weapon that chilled him with an unholy fear.

A shaven skull, ridged with layers of yellow fat, receded from sunken pig eyes, a flattened nose, an underslung jaw. A cauliflower ear sprouted on one side of the head, where the other ear should have been there was nothing. A short-sleeved open shirt exposed a reddish fur-like growth on immensely thick arms and chest. He seemed to be kneeling in the road for the obscenely naked head, thrust forward a bit, was on a level with the steering wheel.

Now the misshapened monster made a curt, beckoning motion with the automatic. "Out!"

When shock still held Manuel motionless the man deftly transferred the gun to his left hand, then hooked prehensile fingers over Manuel's belt. A grunt, and the one hundred and sixty pounds of Manuel Ortega jackknifed, cleared the space between the wheel and seat and catapulted from the car as if sucked out by some tremendous vacuum.

The road met Manuel with pain-numbing impact, jarring breath out of his body. He rolled over within the narrow space between the flanked cars, came to his knees, dazedly shook his head. He could hear the sound of the car motors idling. A man coughed and somebody said something in a language he couldn't understand.

Looking up, he found himself facing the one-eared brute. The man had not been kneeling, as Manuel had thought. He was a monstrosity, a freak of nature, with the torso of a hulking giant attached to the short, curved legs of a dwarf. The abnormality was further accentuated by criss-crossed cartridge belts around his waist, supporting two holstered automatics. The holsters dangled well below his knees.

Another man, now calmly lighting a cigarette, stood near him. He had Manuel's broad-cheeked, copper-hued Indian features but was older. He was dressed in a light gray sombrero, white shirt buttoned at the throat, and neatly pressed chinos. There was an air of gentle frailness about him that seemed out of character with the heavy revolver hanging at his hip.

Glancing left, Manuel saw a third man watching him from the front seat of the sedan. He wore a beret and dark glasses. A neck scarf was pulled up so that it concealed his mouth and chin. Beyond him the figure of a fourth man could be made out, slouched behind the wheel.

Suddenly Manuel turned as he heard a shuffling sound—too late to twist away from the vicious kick in the stomach that sent him sprawling back across the road.

"Up!" the dwarf's guttural voice ordered. "*Levántese!*"

Manuel struggled to a standing position, swaying slightly, one hand pressing his side. He panted, speaking aloud to himself. "I mocked at the Old One, but she knew. *Caray,* how she knew!"

The dwarf edged menacingly closer, to be stopped by the frail, thin man in the grey sombrero. "*Esperete,* Pepe!" In the same commanding tone he went on, now addressing Manuel. "What is it you say, hombre? Who knew what?"

"The grandmother of my wife," Manuel said. "*Una bruja, se dicen.* Very old and blind, she sits and dreams in another world. But sometimes she speaks. Tonight at supper she spoke out of the corner where we thought she was sleeping. 'Manuelito,' she said. 'Do not drive the *americano* this night. There will be bad trouble.' I laughed at her and told her to go back to her dreams." He paused, then added hesitantly, "Is it permitted to ask a foolish question?"

"Ask."

"How bad is the trouble the *viejita* saw in her dreams?"

There was no answer. The night silence was broken only by the sound of the idling motors. Then the dwarfed monster, Pepe, made a sound that was an obscene mockery of a laugh. "Now, Enrico?" he asked. "Is it the time?"

The frail, thin Indio shrugged. "Porque no?"

Pepe reached for the automatic he had holstered. His stubby legs retreated three paces. He bent his arm at a forty-five angle, automatic pointing skyward, the target-range position before starting to fire. Then with tauntingly slow deliberation he began straightening his arm, the muzzle of the gun descending to cover Manuel.

Manuel Ortega closed his eyes. Instinctively his lips moved in wordless prayer. One thought only possessed his mind: he was about to die. His body jerked spasmodically as he heard the shot, the reverberating crash-boom of a .45 at close range. His legs weakened and trembled. But by some miracle they still supported him. He was still on his feet when he heard the sound of the second shot.

He opened his eyes. He saw Pepe's yellow horse-teeth grinning at him. The gun was once again pointed in the air and he heard the sound of the beasts that had been blocking the road lumbering away through the underbrush.

Pepe gave his harsh laugh again. "It is a cool night, yet our brave friend sweats. Perhaps he has the fever, no?"

From the front seat of the big sedan the man wearing the beret and dark glasses spoke curtly, his Spanish foreign-accented. "Your humor ceases to amuse, Pepe. There is no time for it. Bring the man here. You, Enrico, understand your instructions?"

"Si, señor."

"Do not worry yourself," Pepe informed Manuel. "Enrico will carry out your duties without fail. Your americano will be met most promptly."

Suddenly, with a quick sweep of a powerful arm, he sent Manuel stumbling toward the big sedan. Behind him, Manuel heard a car door slam and gears mesh as Enrico drove off.

Then he was being pushed into the rear seat of the big sedan. Pepe shoved against him, overwhelming him with a sour stench of animal sweat. With a powerful throb of motor, the big black sedan moved on.

Jammed into a corner, Manuel tried to fathom a reason for what was happening. It was without logic. His first quick suspicion that he had been waylaid by car thieves he had dismissed. Only fools would involve themselves in stealing a car owned by such a powerful foreign country as los Estados Unidos—and these men were not fools. Evil men, but not stupid.

Pepe now reached down and picked up a bottle from the floor of the car. Removing the cork with his teeth, he held out the bottle. "Drink, my fear-sweating friend."

Suspecting he knew not what, Manuel declined. "Gracias, no. No tome nada."

Pepe leaned forward, addressing the men on the front seat. "He doesn't drink. Think you we have *un maricón* with us?"

"I am no fairy," Manuel protested with dignity. "My wife, Carmelita, and I now have fifty-eight days of marriage. And she is with child."

Without turning his head, the man in the beret said, "Give him to drink."

Pepe's massive hand reached for Manuel's knee. It rested there a moment, then with thumb extended slid along the inside of the thigh. The thumb suddenly jabbed into Manuel's groin as Pepe's fingers tightened in a vise-like grip.

Manuel cried out, half rising with arching back at the excruciating pain.

Easing the pressure, Pepe again extended the bottle. "It is good what you are married. Now you can drink to your wife. First to her eyes."

Certain that the drink would be his last one, Manuel obeyed. He took the bottle, tipped it up, felt raw aguardiente burn down his throat.

"*Bueno*," Pepe said. "And now again. This time to your Carmelita's breasts."

The gouging thumb and vise-like fingers prompted instant obedience. Once again Manuel tilted the bottle to his mouth. When he attempted to hand it back, Pepe mocked at him. "Your wife is not an oddity, is she? Has she not two breasts like all women? Drink to both of them!"

They want me drunk for some reason, Manuel told himself. But why? It is not needful to get a man drunk to kill him in cold blood. He held the bottle to his lips without swallowing but Pepe out-guessed him. Placing spatulate fingers around Manuel's throat he warned, "Do not try to fool me, *cabron.* A long drink now—until I tell you to stop."

Manuel held the bottle up, pouring the aguardiente down his throat until he gagged and the fiery white rum spewed out, dribbling down over his chin.

"Again!" Pepe ordered.

"I shall be sick—"

"It is enough," the man in the beret cut in from the front seat. "I want the rum in his stomach, not in the stink of his vomit."

Some blind and senseless will to defy the strange man giving orders in a foreign accent prompted Manuel to take another drink. A long one. His stomach retched but held. Only his head seemed to be without control, spinning dizzily.

"*Pendejos!*" he muttered. "*Cabrónes sin vergüenza ...*"

Then he sagged over in a drunken stupor.

In the patio of the old baroque residence on the Avenida Bolivar that now housed the United States Embassy, Hobart Drake paced restlessly back and forth. Every few minutes he paused and in the pale yellow light sifting down from the ornate wrought iron lanterns set at intervals high up on the patio walls glanced impatiently at his watch.

Now he did it again, and once again wondered irritably what had happened to Ortega and the car. The man knew he was a stickler for punctuality, yet already he was nearly ten minutes late. The typical Latin attitude toward time and responsibility! True, there was still plenty of time to make the twenty kilometer drive out to the airport at Punta Helvos before the Lima to Miami plane put down briefly at midnight. But that wasn't the point. Hobart Drake hated delay of any kind. Particularly tonight.

Drake was a tall, thin young man, prematurely bald and with a pale, elongated student's face. Family connections within the State Department and an excellent academic record at Princeton had paved his way into the Foreign Service. That had been some six years ago, and at that time he had harbored private dreams of becoming a career diplomat in places like London and Paris and Rome. Instead he had been shunted from one Central American banana republic to another, finally ending up to vegetate in San Barrios as merely another undersecretary in the United States Embassy. A place where nothing ever happened.

Or so he had thought when first he was transferred to San Barrios to serve under the newly-appointed ambassador, Roger Hammet. Then a number of things had happened. Then had come the debacle of the abortive Cuban invasion and the open emergence of Castro's Soviet-backed dictatorship. Both were blows to United States prestige. And in the aftermath, curious and subtly invidious moves began to take place in San Barrios, all serving to seriously sabotage certain highly secret United States plans for that country.

Roger Hammet, the new ambassador, worried and fretted over his inability to control events. That much Hobart Drake quickly discovered. And shortly, by sheer accident, he discovered something else—something that at first shocked him, then frightened him by its ugly implications, and finally forced him into the questionable move he was now making.

That, in large part, was what heightened his impatience now to get away. Uncertainty still nagged him. That he was playing with dynamite he well knew. Suppose—just suppose his strong suspicions and the isolated, fragmentary facts he had dug up to support them all added up to no more than a horrible mistake? There would be literally all hell to pay and he could kiss goodbye to any further thought of a career in public service.

For the hundredth time he tried to evaluate dispassionately exactly what it was that he had to report to the very highest personage he could contact in Washington. Some of it was specific, much of it vaguely intangible. That was why the report had to be made in person. It had to be verbal, not written. Titus Banning was the one man to see short of the President himself.

If, that is, Manuel ever showed up with the car. Drake started to glance at his watch again. And then headlights suddenly bathed the street outside, the Embassy car coasted to a stop.

Hobart Drake picked up his suitcase and hurried toward the patio gate. He swung it open and silently closed it behind him. As he crossed the sidewalk the driver got out of the car, walked around it and opened the rear door for him.

Drake saw with sharp annoyance that it wasn't Manuel but a stranger—a frail, thin man neatly dressed in white shirt and carefully pressed chinos, now standing holding a grey sombrero in one hand.

Before Drake could voice the impatient question that rose to his lips the strange driver became voluble with explanations. A thousand pardons for the delay, *jefe.* It had been unavoidable. His cousin, Manuel Ortega, had been taken suddenly sick. *Una cosa de su estómago.* He had tried the tea of herbs and even medicina from the botica, but nothing had helped. Hence he, Enrico Aguilar, would drive the señor Drake to the airport.

Brusquely Hobart Drake cut the explanations short as he settled himself in the car. As they drove off he turned, glancing through the rear window up at the lights burning in Roger Hammet's private suite on the second floor of the embassy. Perhaps Hammet was working late, as he did so often lately. Perhaps he was enjoying a period of pleasant relaxation with his beautiful wife, Claire.

And perhaps he was simply worrying. He had good cause to worry, Drake reminded himself. Very good cause.

They drove on. Here and there helmeted soldiers, armed with rifles, patrolled the nearly deserted streets, enforcing the curfew imposed because of recent bloody riots. Then they were through the town, through the outskirts of 'dobe huts with thatched roofs. Beyond was the curving stretch of mountainous road, dropping sharply towards the flat, lush lowlands.

They rode in silence. Presently the full moon reflected on water as the road began skirting the shore of Lago Cristóbal, a lake one hundred miles long and fifty miles wide, which together with the rio Dulce, which it fed, practically bisected San Barrios.

The river, deep and navigable, emptied into the Caribbean Sea. Only a twelve-mile land area separated the western edge of the lake from the broad expanse of the Pacific. It was this unique feature of the otherwise insignificant republic of San Barrios that had caused that country to be carefully coddled for over half a century by the United States—and at times secretly eyed with varying degrees of wary speculation by other world powers. For a canal cut through that twelve-mile stretch would link the

Atlantic and Pacific with a navigable waterway more practical and vastly more efficient than that provided by the now inadequate Panama Canal.

Drake's mind was on this specific point when he became aware that the car was suddenly braking to a stop. He looked up. Fifty yards ahead, just short of a sharp turn, a big dusty sedan was parked diagonally across the road. Its headlights skimmed the surface of Lago Cristóbal, shimmering beyond the flimsy wooden safety rail.

Enrico started up the car again, drove to within a few yards of the parked sedan. This time when he stopped Drake demanded impatiently, "Well—what is it? What's wrong?"

Enrico got out of the car without answering. He stood by the car in an attitude of waiting. Then Drake saw the rear door of the big sedan swing open. A short monstrosity of a figure got out, reached in the car and pulled out the body of a man. Holding it easily in his arms, the stubby-legged creature walked slowly towards the car in which Drake waited.

Once again Drake demanded, "What goes on? Has there been an accident?"

This time Enrico answered. He opened the rear door of the car, said quietly, "You will now move to the front seat, señor." And when Drake hesitated, he gestured briefly over his shoulder. "You can see for yourself that it is most necessary."

Protesting, Drake nevertheless obeyed. "I'm sorry if a man has been hurt. Later you can drive him back to the hospital in Colima if need be. Right now it is imperative that I reach the airport in time to make connections with my plane."

Enrico said politely, "Si, señor."

Then the door on the driver's side opened and Drake watched with astonishment now tinged with nervous apprehension as the monstrous half-dwarf eased his limp burden behind the wheel. A strong odor of raw rum made Drake's nose twitch in revulsion. He cried out in disgust, "This man is drunk! Get him out of here immediately!"

"But how otherwise would your man be in a position to drive?" a voice asked in precise but curiously accented English. "That is understandable, is it not, señor Drake?"

Drake turned his head quickly. A man wearing a beret, dark sun-glasses and a scarf concealing his mouth and chin was sliding into the rear seat.

Drake swallowed and his voice when it came sounded thin and cracked to his own ears. "What is the meaning of this? I demand an explanation!"

"Then ask it of your driver."

For the first time Drake saw that the man lolling beside him in a drunken stupor was Manuel Ortega. He cringed away, said loudly, "If this is a joke, I don't appreciate it! I shall see to it that my Embassy lodges a very strong protest—"

"Ah, yes. Your Embassy," the strange voice cut in smoothly, still speaking in English. "Most interesting that you should mention it. I believe that you plan to leave for Washington tonight to discuss certain matters affecting your Embassy. I most strongly advise against it. Such flights are apt to prove most unhealthy."

"I don't know what you're talking about!"

"No? That is indeed most unfortunate. For it means that you have nothing with which to bargain."

In desperation Drake clutched at the offered straw. "I didn't say that."

"Then you do have important information to offer?"

"You should know," Drake said. "You should most certainly know. For now I recognize your voice."

"Ah, yes. I suspected that you would." The man in the beret sighed. "You are a very smart man, señor Drake, in certain small ways. And very much of a fool in other matters. It is a failing that my servant, Pepe, will now correct."

Drake was belatedly aware that the dwarf-monster had slid onto the rear seat and was leaning toward him. Hands like steel tentacles suddenly reached out to clamp about his head, thumbs seeking and pressing relentlessly on the pressure points that checked the blood flow to the brain. Drake moaned. His body thrashed wildly, his hands pawing futilely at hairy arms of iron. His tongue thickened in his mouth and there was a roaring sound in his ears. Then merciful oblivion as he was sucked down into a vortex of blackness.

Meanwhile the driver of the big sedan had maneuvered his car around until it was behind the Embassy car, bumper to bumper. Pepe and the man in the beret got out and stood by the side of the road. The latter made a quick gesture of readiness and the sedan surged ahead with a throaty roar of power, pushing the Embassy car with increasing speed towards the sharp bend in the road.

There was the sound of splintering wood as the car carrying the two unconscious men crashed through the safety rail. For a brief moment the car seemed air-borne, then there was a geyser-like upsurge of water as the car plunged into the black depths of Lago Cristóbal.

The man in the beret and dark glasses walked slowly over to the edge of the lake bank and directed the beam of a flashlight downward. Only the very top of the car was blackly visible above the water, like some rectangular turtle coming to surface. Air bubbles rose briefly to break the now glassy smoothness. Then nothing.

The man nodded, permitting himself a fleeting smile of satisfaction at a job neatly done, and returned silently to the waiting car.

CHAPTER ONE

BART GOULD stretched out on the rub-down table, eyes shut, relaxing fully as Jodey's skilled fingers kneaded his lean, rope-muscled body. Ten years before Jodie Harris had been a promising middleweight contender, only to run afoul of the underworld bosses who control boxing. He had insisted stubbornly on winning one night when he should have lost. Twelve hours later he had been picked up more dead than alive, a dozen stab wounds in his body, on a city dump on the outskirts of New York. Gould had heard the story and sought him out, creating the fictitious job of physical trainer and masseur.

The ring set up in the basement of Gould's Washington home had just been the scene of a fast five round workout, followed by twenty quick laps of the pool. Now Gould lay limp, drowsy with healthy fatigue.

"What's that?" he bestirred himself to ask sleepily, aware that Jodey had spoken.

"I was just kind of talking to myself, Mister Bart. Saying that you sure got the damnedest mess of old scars I ever seen on one body. And I was just wondering like how a gentleman like you ever come by them."

"Over the years," Gould murmured lazily. "Over the years and one by one. Such things just happen."

Did they just happen, he asked himself now, or had he subconsciously gone looking for them? With a touch of wry, objective amusement he began tabulating the near-brushes with death that were now permanently logged as scars on his body. The Chinese sniper's bullet that had creased his ribs, just missing his heart, the time he was leading a commando raid in North Korea. The horn of a maddened rhino in Kenya that had seared his hip bone. The long, livid scar down one leg that was a lasting memento of the time he was trying for the French Grand Prix at Rheims and took the first curve, the Courbe de Gueux, at too much over the safe 100 miles an hour. His Ferrari had crashed and burned but by some miracle he had been thrown clear. The ugly marks on his thigh, reminder of an experience with a hammerhead shark while deep-sea diving for sunken treasure along the coast of Yucatan Channel.

Then Gould's wry amusement stopped suddenly when without conscious intention he thought of the ten-year-old scar that was invisible and had never healed. The lovely girl who had died in a plane crash just a week before their scheduled marriage. That had spawned the subsequent restlessness and recklessness—the constant flirtation with danger in the far corners of the earth, and in the sky and sea as well. That, in large part, was what had brought about his public reputation as a millionaire playboy-sportsman-adventurer.

And now, at 36, he felt bored and jaded.

He sat up abruptly, said shortly, "That will be enough, Jodie." As Jodie stepped back, his brown face impassive, Gould felt a twinge of guilt. Because he felt impatient with himself he had no business taking it out on others who couldn't answer back. He said, "Sorry, Jodie, if I seem short."

"It's okay, Mister Bart."

Gould slid off the table, slipped his arms through the terry cloth robe Jodie held out, crossed over to the waiting elevator. The small cage ascended quietly.

On the third floor the elevator door opened directly into the study adjoining the master's bedroom. The Explorer's Club would have envied—indeed, had envied more than once in the past—the large, comfortably appointed room dominated by a huge field-stone fireplace at one end. The deep club chairs were of honestly worn leather in deep russets and forest green, the large tables and incidental pieces of darkly gleaming mahogany. At present the panelled walls were hung with numerous horns and heads that were trophies of various African hunts, each a prime exhibit of its type. There was a giant forest boar from equatorial Africa, a black rhino from near Kilimanjaro, a black-maned lion from Somaliland, ibex from the Red Sea hills and addax from Dongola. Each one sought out in the locale in which it attained its fullest glory.

Over the desk in a far corner were a few other framed mementos. The Ferrari before it crashed and burned at Rheims. His fifty-foot ketch, Mariposa, now riding at anchor near the old homestead up on Cape Cod. The framed citation explaining why Major Bartholomew Gould, of the United States Marine Corps, had been awarded the Congressional Medal of Honor.

As Gould paused now to glance around the room a frown crossed his lean, hawk-like face. He had the depressing feeling that there was something fraudulent about the place. It was a testimonial to *past* achievements—if it were meant to suggest an adventurous spirit flexing its muscles, then it was outdated. Such a spirit no longer existed.

He sighed, then crossed over to the serving bar at one side of the fireplace and poured himself an inch of *ron negrito*. He took a small sip, savouring the taste of the heavy, dark rum. He opened a box, took out a long, thin cigarette of straight Havana leaf wrapped in wheatstraw, made to his special order by a famous old New York firm. "I'm old-fashioned," he sometimes explained to close friends who questioned his extreme tastes. "I like cigarettes that taste like tobacco, drinks that taste like real liquor, and women who are completely feminine." Then he would laugh to take the sting out of his words. "Three things increasingly hard to find in this synthetic age."

Gould sat down now on the arm of a club chair, trying without success to make his mind a comfortable blank. That was when Hobbs, the aging butler whom he had inherited along with the Washington house from his grandfather, flamboyant old Senator Gould, who had been the political and social maverick of his era, entered from the bedroom.

"It's time for you to dress, sir. Black tie or tails?"

Gould hesitated, then shook his head.

Hobbs ignored the gesture. "There is a small affair at the French Legation, as well as a reception at the Danish Embassy. And Mrs. Lafritz telephoned earlier to remind you of her supper-dance."

"Good old Dolly," Gould said. "Always reminding somebody of something." He stood up and put down his empty glass. "I haven't decided yet what I want to do. Only what I don't want to do, and that includes listening to more Washington gossip. If I'm not careful the day will come when I believe some of it." He favored the old butler with a small grin and pulled an affectionate nickname out of the far past. "You don't have to wait around for me to decide, Hobbsie. I'll manage to make out for myself."

Alone again, Gould poured himself another *ron negrito.* His annoyance with himself hadn't lessened. He knew what was wrong—had known, actually, for weeks. It was simply that the adventurous escapism for which he had trained his body and his nerves no longer held any appeal.

So now what? Frankly he didn't know the answer although he was only too aware of an inner restlessness that threatened to explode at any minute.

Meanwhile there were the immediate empty hours ahead to be filled. A good dinner with the right wines followed by some decent brandy, either a Polignac or Fundador would do, might lift his mood. But not if he sat in brooding solitude. Fortunately there was always one pleasant diversion with which to correct this loneliness. He crossed over to the telephone table, settled down and took a small Florentine leather address book from the drawer.

Only certain numbers were listed—those of the most beautiful and amorously talented young women in Washington. A few were admitted call girls, the tops in their profession. But the majority were women, many socially prominent, with a decided flair for sexual adventures providing they could find a discreet and equally sophisticated partner. Gould idly flicked the pages. He paused at the name of the Italian countess who never ceased to amaze him with her erotic knowledge and sensual tricks. But, no—she would probably be at the French Legation affair tonight. So, too, in all probability would be Lady Fairchild, the pale, cool blonde Englishwoman who looked like a statuette carved in ice and became a searing ember of fire in bed. Under the circumstances, the night seemed made for one of the call girls. That was better, in a way, for afterwards there could be no social complications.

The telephone rang even as he reached for it. Hobbs' voice came from the master phone below. "Mr. Titus Banning wishes to speak to you, sir."

"Banning?" Gould frowned in faint puzzlement. "Put him on."

A moment and the clipped, slightly nasal New England tones of Titus Banning came over the wire. " 'Evening, Gould. Can you arrange to be free for the next hour?"

"I presume so."

"Good. A car will pick you up in—" There was a minute pause. "—in exactly twenty-two minutes."

There was a click and the line went dead. Automatically Gould glanced at the desk clock. It was precisely 6:18. He looked back at the phone, his puzzled frown deepening. What the hell could this be all about? He knew him. Former governor of a small New England state, and former senator, the man was famous—or infamous, according to one's viewpoint—for his dry mannerisms, his impatience with waste of time or money, his razor-sharp mind. He was now a key figure of power in the new administration, with an office in the White House, although his exact position had never been clearly defined for the public record.

He must have some bee buzzing in his bonnet now, but Gould was damned if he could imagine what.

He recalled the last brief encounter—if it even could be called that—he had had with Banning. That had been several nights before at a reception given by the Brazilian Embassy, an affair considered of particular importance in view of Brazil's newly adopted form of government following the temperamental walk-out of Jânio Quadros. There was an over-abundance of Brazilian champagne and brandy flowing.

During the evening Cliff Ramsdell, of the Securities Exchange Commission, had cornered Gould with the information that he was planning to spend his vacation on a big game hunt in Kenya. He had suggested that Gould join him.

Gould had declined. Then, when Ramsdell had persisted in his invitation, he had let the inspiration of too much brandy take over and had said half-jokingly, half-seriously, "I don't get a kick out of an organized safari any more. A bit too one-sided. The only sort of game I would like to stalk now—and be stalked by, in return—would be a human adversary. A deadly enemy, with craft and cunning. A hunt where the delicate balance of kill-or-be-killed wasn't affected by mere chance but by out-thinking and out-guessing the other."

Before he could continue he heard a grunt behind him. Glancing over his shoulder, Gould found himself looking into Titus Banning's frosty blue eyes. Banning had nodded with curt briefness, then wordlessly turned on his heel and walked away.

Remembering the incident, Gould gave his head a quick shake. Certainly there had been nothing in that fleeting encounter to explain Banning's curious telephone call. Summons would be a better word, Gould now decided, and glanced again at the time.

Exactly four minutes had passed.

Gould got up and went into his bedroom and started dressing.

CHAPTER TWO

THERE WERE no delays.

Promptly at 6:40 an anonymous looking black limousine chauffeured by an anonymous looking driver pulled up in front of the Gould residence.

Bart Gould was ready. He stepped out of his front door, walked briskly to the waiting car and got in, settling back as though being summoned to the White House at a moment's notice were an everyday affair. He had given up trying to puzzle out what might be in Banning's mind. Now he let his thoughts dwell on the man who now officially occupied the White House. To Gould's precise knowledge the President was his elder by nine years and eight months. Curiously, even as a boy, the difference in years hadn't seemed too great. Thinking back on those summers, Gould smiled wryly to himself. The President would have little time now for teaching a gangling youth how to develop a decent backhand at tennis or perform an adequate jackknife or backflip.

The heavy congestion of late afternoon Washington traffic that followed the closing of government offices had thinned somewhat. As the car turned down Pennsylvania Avenue, Gould noticed the scudding clouds that were cutting short the twilight hour. If it rained it would raise hell with Dolly Lafritz's party, he thought, and congratulated himself on deciding not to go.

He wondered once more what Banning wanted.

Titus Banning's White House office came very close to being a caricature of the public image of the man. The furnishings were sparse to the point of bleakness. A battered roll-top desk set against one wall. A number of scarred, wooden arm chairs. A tree rack in one corner on which a suit coat of pepper-and-salt material was hanging.

The only modern note was a bank of telephones on a table flanking the roll-top desk.

Titus Banning was speaking on one of the telephones as Gould was shown in. Which meant that in the main he was confining himself to noncommittal grunts while he scribbled cryptic notes on a legal pad. Finally he said crisply, "Very well, I'll see that the matter is taken up directly with the President." He cradled the phone, picked up another and pressed a button. "No more calls until I say so."

Finally he spun around in his swivel chair and faced Gould. "Sit down. This may take a little time."

I'm as much of a New Englander as you, Gould said silently. I can play the same salty game. He sat down and waited.

"You wonder why you're here?"

"No." Gould shook his head. "Figure you'll tell me." Banning's frosty blue eyes gave him a searching look. Then he reached over on his desk and picked up a folder stamped in big block letters CONFIDENTIAL. He held it up, then dropped it back on the desk. "Report on you. Routine. Nothing in it I didn't know myself."

Gould managed to keep his face expressionless.

Banning went on. "Main thing right now is this. Your great-uncle, Colonel Mathias Gould, commanded the Marine forces sent to the Republic of San Barrios some forty years ago to quell internal disorders, protect American interests, and train the local army. When the Marines were withdrawn in 1925 your great-uncle, having reached retirement age, returned to San Barrios, settled down as a private citizen and made a number of very lucrative investments which you inherited at his death."

Gould contented himself with nodding.

"Investments that are still extremely valuable," Banning went on. "Two coffee fincas, a large stretch of timberland, mining concessions. More to the point, you are passably familiar with the country. As a boy you spent a full year there on your uncle's hacienda after being suspended from prep school for certain—ah—precocious activities involving a chorus girl. You have made several brief visits since then."

Gould didn't know whether to be amused or annoyed. "Your report didn't miss much."

"It wasn't supposed to. Now then, after some thirty years of stability, San Barrios is suddenly beset with internal political troubles. Anti-government riots, anti-*yanqui* demonstrations, all the rest. Plus demands to expropriate foreign-owned properties. Alvarez, the *presidente,* claims it is all just talk that he can control. That's as may be." Banning hesitated momentarily, focused his attention on the sleeve of his alpaca office jacket, then looked up. "Point is, as one of the foreign property owners who might be affected you have good reason to go down there and see what's what."

So far Bart Gould's attitude had been one of polite interest. Now he suddenly stiffened. "Wait a minute! With all due respect, I have no intention of going to San Barrios to pull anybody's financial chestnuts out of the fire. My own included. That sort of outside interference just plays into the hands of the local rabble-rousers for one thing, and for another it's damned poor policy these days. I should think you'd learned your lesson in Cuba."

Banning held up a thin, scrawny hand and Gould stopped, a little ashamed of his outburst. Banning said evenly, "Don't jump to conclusions, please. I simply said you had a good reason to go to San Barrios. An excuse. Personally," he said, with a touch of his famous asperity, "I don't give a tinker's damn what happens to your holdings in San Barrios. Or elsewhere. There are far more important fish to fry right now."

"Such as?"

"The immediate future of our country. The destruction of a vital strategic base. A possible anti-American uprising in Latin America leading to war."

Titus Banning paused, as though to let his quietly spoken words sink in, then went on in the same dry, precise tone, "Let me remind you of a few things you probably know. Or should know. San Barrios, although relatively insignificant in itself, has for many years had great potential importance to the United States. The world's biggest liner, or battleship, can enter from the Caribbean Sea into the mouth of a deeply navigable river, traverse the river and enter the hundred-mile long Lago Cristóbal. Only a twelve-mile land barrier blocks final passage to the Pacific. Always was the most feasible route for a canal linking the two oceans. Still is."

"Unfortunately, when the project was first broached England, for regrettably short-sighted reasons of its own, managed to block the business. The result was that we got involved in the Panama Canal. Always less efficient and practical, and today even more so. Worse, with its cumbersome system of locks it is susceptible to sabotage by any crack-pot with a mind to do so."

Once again Banning paused. Bart Gould shifted slightly in the uncomfortable wooden armchair, wondering at the purpose behind this bit of ancient history.

Titus Banning seemed to read his mind. "I am just making sure you understand the background fully. Possibly you are also aware that we have a treaty with San Barrios, negotiated in 1916 and still in effect today, which gives us the right to build a canal. Fine on the face of it. But we have outlived the era when such a treaty could be enforced by arms, if need be. Now such a document, no matter how legal, only has meaning *if* the government in power is friendly to the United States."

More puzzled than ever, Gould evinced an opinion for the first time. "It seems to me you are outlining a problem that belongs to our State Department or Defense Department. Why should I be told about it?"

"Let me finish, if you don't mind. Plans have already been formulated for going ahead with the San Barrios canal. In secret, as far as such things are possible. Physical work on breaking through the land block—tunnels, excavations, and the like—to be done under the pretext of mining operations. A crash program that will be completed before it can be talked to death."

Gould said carefully, "Sounds like a good idea."

"It *was* a good idea. Now the plans are no longer secret. Somebody else knows them. There have been threats. Ugly ones. As you may know, there is a special meeting of the O.A.S., called to ratify highly important inter-American defense plans, scheduled for the 27th of this month. That is exactly nine days from now. The meeting will take place in Colima, San Barrios. We have been threatened that unless we immediately recall our present ambassador to San Barrios, unless we drop once and for all our plans for a canal across that country, certain drastic things will happen. First off, on the very stroke of the hour that the O.A.S. meeting opens a sabotage attempt will be made on the Panama Canal. As a result, in obvious self-protection, we will have to send in additional military forces to occupy the Canal Zone. Such a move would seriously worsen our bargaining position with President Chiari in working out a revision of the canal treaties that Panama now demands. Next, we have been threatened that there will be a small, unsuccessful anti-government uprising in San Barrios itself, consisting in the main of men wearing U.S. army uniforms and carrying U.S. weapons. We will, in short, be clearly and publicly held up to the world as an aggressor nation making unprovoked attacks on our good neighbors for imperialistic ends. In a matter of hours we may well find ourselves trapped in a series of little shooting wars that can turn out to be ten times worse than Korea."

Banning stopped abruptly as though to lend further emphasis to his final words.

Bart Gould sat forward in his chair and asked the obvious question. "Who is this *somebody* who knows our secrets? Who is making these threats?"

Pursing his thin lips, Titus Banning stared back at Gould for a long moment. His words, when they came, were bitten off sharply as though he begrudged each one. "We don't know. And that, Mr. Gould, is the reason you are here."

CHAPTER THREE

"WHY ME?" Bart Gould asked again.

"Because the President decided that this was a one-man job. There isn't time to utilize the usual agencies. Besides, we can't have C.I.A. men and G.2 men swarming all over the place, getting in one another's way. We can't even afford to take official cognizance of these threats. Too dangerous for our prestige. The business has to be handled by an individual *completely on his own!*"

Gould leaned forward, lines of concentrated interest now marking his hawk-like face. "Sounds to me as though you were suggesting a man hunt."

"I am."

"I suppose it has occurred to you that these threats you refer to are just the work of some crack-pot without any solid backing?"

"Naturally." Titus Banning's voice became more tartly New Englandish. "Contrary to some of the public press we know our business here." He reached over on his desk, picked up another folder. "Just four nights ago there was an unfortunate—" He paused as though taking time to pick the exact word. "—occurrence in San Barrios. The car carrying Hobart Drake, an under-secretary to our embassy in San Barrios, to the airport at Punta Helvos ran off the road and plunged into Lago Cristóbal. Both Drake and the embassy chauffeur, one Manuel Ortega, were drowned."

Gould said, "I know that stretch of road. It's tricky but not particularly dangerous."

"Quite. It was put down as an accident. An autopsy, insisted on by our people, revealed that the driver, Ortega, was drunk."

"That's quite possible. So?"

"Just this. Ortega, by all accounts, was an extremely temperate man. He took great pride in his job with our embassy and wouldn't do anything to jeopardize it. So much for that. Mere hearsay. Hobart Drake, on the other hand, I knew slightly. Extremely conscientious and a stickler for detail. Lived by the rule book. However, the morning of his intended departure from San Barrios he sent a wire to me at my home requesting an immediate private interview on arrival. Unusual procedure for a man of Drake's type."

"If it's the same Hobart Drake I knew at Princeton, I agree."

Banning nodded. "Drake was a Princeton man. Now then, after his untimely death another curious fact came to light. Drake naturally asked permission to leave his post for a short trip to the States. That permission was readily granted when he explained to our Ambassador, Roger Hammet, that he had just received word that his mother was seriously ill."

Gould started to ask a question and then waited.

Banning said, "I call that curious, Mr. Gould, for one simple reason. As I say, I knew Drake slightly. Knew his family when I was younger. He was an only child and both his mother and father died some twenty years ago."

For a long moment there was silence in the bleakly furnished White House office. Finally Gould asked softly, "Just what are you suggesting?"

"Murder, Mr. Gould," Titus Banning said. "And you may believe me that that is not a word I use lightly."

⚜ ⚜ ⚜

Bart Gould leaned forward, slate-gray eyes narrowed thoughtfully. He was beginning to feel the inner keenness, the anticipatory tingle of nerves, that a challenge had always excited in the old days.

He said, "One more thing. You mentioned that certain secrets had been stolen from our embassy in San Barrios. You have definite proof?"

"Unfortunately, yes. We were sent a microfilm copy of some of the documents. Moreover, Hammet admits there must have been some incredible laxity on his part. He offered to resign." Titus Banning placed the tips of his fingers neatly together, studied them for a moment, then glanced up. "Roger Hammet, as you should know, is not the usual political hack of the type past administrations were in the habit of sending down to the banana republics. He is a professor of political economy who has specialized in Latin American affairs. Most of his books have been translated into Spanish and well received. He enjoys an excellent reputation south of the border. He was personally selected for the San Barrios post by the President. I might add that there was considerable opposition in the Senate, led by the usual rightwing obstructionist bloc. Naturally the President is standing by him now."

Gould nodded, his mind busy sorting out and analysing all he had heard since entering this ultra-private office. When at last he spoke it was slowly, deliberately. "Let me make sure I understand. You are suggesting that I go down to San Barrios, track down this mysterious person who threatens our security, and somehow deal with him."

"Not *somehow*," Banning corrected. "Effectively is the word."

Gould gave a short laugh. "I know of only one way of dealing effectively with a menace. Remove it!"

This time Titus Banning didn't answer. Simply looked back at him with expressionless eyes.

"I see," Gould said. "I really begin to see." He felt a wave of anger rising within him, as it always did when someone took too much about him for granted. "And what gave you the bright idea of getting me to be your private *pistolero*?"

"Not my idea at all." Banning glanced up at the ceiling. "I have only one job here—that is to take orders and suggestions and see that they are carried out quickly and efficiently. I was told to get hold of you and to explain the problem. Thoroughly. When I protested that it might be imprudent to give you so much sensitive information without knowing what your reaction might be, I was assured by the man I work for that you wouldn't refuse any dangerous assignment if it served your country." Once again Banning reached over on his desk, this time picking up a manila envelope. "In fact, so positive was he of your acceptance of the mission that certain arrangements have already been made. In an hour a private plane will fly you over to Idlewild, in New York. Passage has already been booked for you on the Air France jet taking off at midnight for Mexico City. There you will change to a plane that will put you down in Punta Helvos. You will find your tickets and other essential information here."

Bart Gould drew a deep breath. "It doesn't look as though I had much choice, does it?"

As Banning started to answer, the office door behind Gould opened. Gould saw Titus Banning get to his feet, heard him say, "Good-evening, Mr. President."

Then, before Bart Gould could turn, he heard the old, familiar voice that carried him back to the vacation days of his boyhood saying, "Hello, Bart. I just dropped in to wish you luck on your little trip. Come back healthy and I'll wallop you again at tennis." The note of studied lightness suddenly trailed off. "If I ever find time for such things again …"

CHAPTER FOUR

DAWN BROKE brief minutes after the stop at Tegucigalpa. As the plane swept down over the curving coastline of Honduras and Nicaragua, Bart Gould turned a preoccupied glance at a distant mass of clouds, extravagantly tinted by the rays of a sun still hidden below the far horizon of the Caribbean. His mind was busy with the problem ahead—busy at the same time trying to digest the information given him in Washington the night before.

Now that he was away from Titus Banning's presence, no longer subject to the influence of that authoritative New England voice, it was difficult to give reality to the business. Bart Gould knew that Washington was over-jittery these days, like a skittish horse inclined to shy at its own shadow. The place was full of rumors and counter-rumors, each one more lurid than the others. Duvalier was supposed to have secretly sold out Haiti to the Russians, who planned to use it as a base for sweeping through the neighboring Dominican Republic and tumbling Ramfis Trujillo from power. Castro was plotting an invasion of Spanish Honduras. In Mexico, old Lazaro Cárdenas was reported to be storing up caches of arms, smuggled in through Yucatan, preparatory to leading an uprising against a government he maintained had sold out to *yanqui* imperialism.

Against this backdrop of melodramatic foreign intrigue it was small wonder that credence should be given to any sort of wild tale coming out of San Barrios. Even to anonymous threats.

But now, smoking his first cigarette of the day over the cup of richly aromatic coffee served by the Panagra stewardess—a blend of Guatemalan and Columbian coffees, his nose decided—Bart Gould wondered just how much of a wild goose chase he might be on.

At the moment there was no way of telling. He summoned the stewardess, learned that her name was Dolores Madero, and requested another cup of coffee. As he watched her sleek hips move gracefully up the aisle he decided that one way or another he would manage to enjoy himself in San Barrios. He had very nearly forgotten how sensuously attractive young Spanish girls can be.

Fifteen minutes later the plane circled for a landing, skimmed down to meet the concrete of one of the central runways with an almost imperceptible bump. As he stepped out of the plane Bart Gould paused, glancing with the wry amusement the spectacle always afforded him at the ornate impressiveness of the airport buildings, suitable for a country ten times the size of San Barrios, that served mainly as a monument to the vanity of old Hector Alvarez, the presidente.

As he moved towards Customs he noticed an unusual number of soldiers in combat uniform stationed about the vast expanse of the air field. Inside the Customs Building the regular immigration officials were augmented by little groups of army officers.

The delays were interminable.

As his passport was re-examined for the fifth time, Gould managed to curb his mounting impatience. With just a faint touch of sarcasm he said, “That is an American passport, in case you haven’t seen one before.”

“It is a matter of security,” one of the younger officers told him stiffly. “May I ask the purpose of your visit to our country?”

"You may. It is a combination of business and pleasure. Among other things I hope to enjoy several visits with an old family friend, your *presidente.*" He leaned over the Immigration desk and tapped the passport. "I suggest that you eliminate further delay by conferring with one of your senior officers who will find the name not unfamiliar."

"There is no need, señor Gould. The delay was unintentional. Simply a matter of—"

"I know." Gould cut him short. "Routine security."

When he reached the baggage counter there was only a cursory inspection of the wardrobe suitcase that was his single piece of luggage. A portador took it in charge, leading the way out through the massive lobby flamboyantly decorated with murals of vividly colored tiles depicting somewhat biased bits of San Barrios history. He got into the first of a short line of waiting taxis, an ancient Dodge sedan, and gave the address of the Palace Hotel.

During the first part of the drive Gould remained lost in thought, trying to decide if the time-consuming delay at Customs had any significance. Immigration and customs officials the world over were subject to fitful waves of officious inefficiency. It could have been no more than that—except that it didn't explain the number of soldiers and officers on duty.

Then as the car started taking the curves bordering Lago Cristóbal, Gould leaned forward and spoke to the driver.

"I understand there was a bad accident near here a few nights ago."

The driver half turned. "Si, señor. At the very next curve. Two men were drowned when their car soared off the road and submerged itself in the lake."

Gould's eyes followed the road ahead. Shortly he saw the repaired safety rail, gleaming with new white paint. Carefully he noted the angle of the immediate curve. He said casually, "A man would have to be driving at great speed to miss so easy a turn."

"It is not that easy, señor, if one dooes not give it close attention. *Y se dicen que Manuel estuvo andando en la uva.* Me, I do not believe it. He was the cousin of my wife, and never have I seen him drunk."

"Then what happened?"

"*Quien sabe?*" The driver shrugged his shoulders. "It is possible that the *norte-americano* who was also drowned was at fault. But how is not known."

Gould didn't pursue the subject. He remained thoughtfully silent until the car pulled up some twenty minutes later in front of the Palace Hotel on Avenida Santiago.

The stucco exterior of the old hotel had been freshly painted in pink and lavender. Otherwise Gould could see no changes from the last time he had stepped inside, some three years ago. The same massive color photographs of old Hector Alvarez stared down from the lobby walls. The same elephant ears drooped greenly in *macetas* placed against the supporting pillars. The same middle-aged clerk whose face always reminded Gould of newly-cured pig skin standing importantly doing nothing behind the marble-topped desk.

He glanced up negligently as Gould approached, then his eyes became nervously alert. "Señor Gould, is it not? We had no idea you were planning to visit us."

"A pleasant surprise, I hope?"

"But certainly." The man's smile struck Gould as being forced. "It is always a pleasure. But if we had only known in advance—"

"You mean you have no vacancies?" Gould cut in sharply.

"For you space can always be found, señor. Although there are so many reservations because of the conference taking place next week—" Suddenly he broke off, losing for a moment his air of nervousness. "Perhaps that is why you are here, señor Gould? Because of the conference?"

"Perhaps," Gould said shortly. "Now how about my room?"

He was given a suite consisting of a small sitting room, an over-sized bedroom and an adjoining bath. It was now shortly after nine o'clock. Gould telephoned down to the dining room, ordered a breakfast of papaya, huevos revueltos con jamón y café con leche sent up. While he waited he stripped and took a tepid shower. He had just finished shaving with the old-fashioned straight edge razor to which he was addicted when the waiter appeared with his breakfast.

He ate slowly, trying to formulate his immediate plans for the day. Facing him was the problem of a man-hunt—with no idea as to the identity of his quarry. No clues. No discernible tracks. But that was only on the surface, Bart Gould reminded himself, his mind going back to his first safaris in Africa. The clues were always there for an eye trained to find them.

One thing was certain. There was a curious tension in the air of San Barrios—a malaise in the body politic. He had sensed it first at the airport, again as he was being driven through the mid-town section of Colima towards the hotel. The people on the street moved with a different tempo from that of their normal Latin exuberance, quickly and almost silently, as though anxious to get off the streets. In a way it reminded him of the un-Latin atmosphere of Trujillo, before the murder of the old dictator, when the sound of laughter was rarely heard in public.

Find out what's going on, he advised himself, and somewhere a clue to the bigger problem might turn up. He decided that the place to start was at the top.

He got up, walked over to the telephone and settled down to make a series of calls. There were delays with the switchboard, more than the usual number of crossed wires. It was several minutes before Gould could get his first call through, one to the presidential palace.

He spoke to a secretary, presented his compliments to His Excellency, requested an opportunity to appear in person. After a florid interchange of Spanish courtesies he was invited to appear at the palace at five-thirty in the afternoon.

Next Gould called the United States Embassy. Again there was a delay in getting through. Finally he spoke to Roger Hammet, made an appointment for one o'clock.

He started next to put through a long-distance call to Guillermo Wagner, the German-Spanish manager of his San Barrios interests, and then for some reason decided against it. Wagner could wait until later.

The time, he saw, was now just a minute shy of ten-thirty. Over two hours to kill before he could start leisurely for the Embassy. He knew now what he wanted to do and that was to get the feel of the city at first hand.

Quickly he finished dressing and went out and walked down the curving staircase from the second floor to the lobby. He tossed his room key onto the marble-topped reservation counter without stopping and went on out through the wide, carved wooden street doors held open by a portero.

He stood for a moment on the sidewalk of Avenida Santiago and then turned left towards the central business section.

In a big, dusty sedan parked across the avenue a man wearing dark glasses and a beret turned his head and spoke briefly to a *mestizo* sitting in the rear seat.

Fingering the knife hidden inside his waistband the man listened, nodded, and slipping out of the car began following Bart Gould.

CHAPTER FIVE

WALKING ALONG the Avenida Santiago, Bart Gould tried once again to pin down the exact nature of the curious tension in the air. On the surface a part of the tension could be put down to the upcoming O.A.S. conference and the need of curbing the communist-fomented demonstrations that inevitably took place at such times.

But there was more to it than that, Gould was somehow certain. Normally, on his return to any Latin-American city, he relaxed in enjoying the sharp contrast between the garishly new and the old. Modern shopfronts of metal and glass flanked ancient buildings of timeworn stone where heavy double doors flung wide led into large, nearly barren but spotlessly clean patios, once private homes that had now been given over to offices and small business enterprises.

There was a preponderance of radio shops, of pastelerias, of book stores. Usually at this mid-morning hour the streets were crowded, a combination of hectic activity and the Latin compulsion to stop and engage in lengthy conversations.

Today there was the same activity but the overtones of conversation were missing. Even the modern young girls, proudly flaunting their curves, seemed less concerned with evoking admiring whistles and comments than usual.

Four blocks from the Palace Hotel the Avenida Santiago circled around the Plaza de Libertad with its inevitable statue of

Hector Álvarez in the center and entered Avenida Colón at an angle.

Colón was the main business street of the capital, boasting in its short length of barely half a mile the city's two rascacielos, one of twelve and the other of fifteen stories.

To celebrate the upcoming conference of the Organization de Estados Americanos, each corner held the flag of one of the South American countries participating. Every few feet small boys, old women and professional street venders waved strips of lottery tickets in Gould's face, hawking the special ten million peso drawing for the 20th of May, two days away. Gould tried to recall the significance of that date in San Barrios history without success. Like most Latin American countries, San Barrios had too many special dates for a foreigner to remember. He yielded to the importunities on an old lady and as he handed over twenty pesos for a vigésimo asked, "Qué pasa en el veinte de Mayo, viejita?"

Small, obsidian eyes flickered over him.

"It is the birthday of our benefactor, el presidente."

"Of course. I had forgotten."

"There are some things one should not forget, señor."

"Tú hablas con razón, viejita." On impulse Gould took another ten peso note from his pocket, thrust into her gnarled fingers. "This is for reminding me."

"Gracias, patrón." She bent her head, adding in a lower voice, "The señor is perhaps aware that he is being followed?"

Gould resisted the impulse to turn. He patted the old one lightly on the shoulder. "You have sharp eyes."

"For what they are worth. Vaya con Dios, señor."

Gould allowed himself to be caught up again in the stream of movement along the sidewalk. Was he really being followed, he wondered, or had it just been a bit of macabre humor on the part of the old lottery ticket seller? And if followed, then by whom? The secret police often took an active interest in strangers, but that shouldn't apply to him. He wasn't exactly a stranger in the country. It made no sense, but neither did the feeling of uneasiness that had oppressed him since his arrival in San Barrios hours before.

He glanced at his watch and came to a sudden decision. There was time enough to drop in at the Diario de Colima. Rubén de la Vega the editor, was an old friend. Possibly he could tell him what accounted for the change in the tempo of the country. At any rate, they could spend a pleasant half hour recounting past escapades.

It was midway down the next block that the girl accosted him. He had been vaguely aware of her walking at his side and then suddenly she swung in front of him, blocking his way. "Señor, un momento, por favor."

He glanced down at her, appreciatively noting a skin the mellow tone of pale amber and the provocative thrust of breasts against the thin dark silk of a form-fitting dress.

"A sus órdenes, señorita."

"You are, perhaps, un norte americano?" She spoke with nervous rapidity as though in a hurry to get the words out. "You are, perhaps, a stranger in our country? It is possible you are lacking in companionship?"

Gould started to answer with casual humor and then became aware that she was not looking at him but over his shoulder. A sixth sense warned him even as she suddenly cried out, "You insult me! I am a decent girl, not a puta of the streets!"

While she was still crying out he took a long step forward and to one side. Spinning about he saw the glint of sunlight on steel even before he fully noted that man who had been standing just behind him. He acted instinctively. He kicked out—the short, power-packed drive that had dropped-kicked many a field goal when he was a Princeton All-American—catching the man on the sensitive inner side of the ankle. His hand shot out, fingers gripping an arm deflected by sudden pain from its purpose. A thin-bladed knife clattered on the sidewalk.

Something struck him from behind, scraping down the side of his face.

He half turned, saw the girl who had accosted him swinging her handbag. His hand caught it in mid-air, wrenched it out of her grasp.

"Pig!" she was screaming. "Gringo murderer! Yanqui scum!"

"Calla-te!" Gould snapped. "What the hell goes on here?"

He reached out to grab her by the shoulders. Suddenly she twisted about, dove through the gathering crowd of curious, disappeared down the street.

Gould turned back to his assailant. He was just in time to see the man being dragged into a dark dust-covered sedan that in the next moment pulled away from the curb and shot into the streaming traffic.

The knife still glittered on the sidewalk. Gould bent down and picked it up. He became aware that he was still holding the girl's handbag, and at the same moment caught the ugly murmur of the crowd that had collected. He moved to the curb, spotted a *libre* cruising by and stepped out into the street to flag it down. Without waiting for the car to roll to a stop he jerked open the door, eased inside. The driver glanced back over his shoulder.

"To the Zócalo," Gould ordered. "Circle around it and come back to the office of the Diario de Colima."

The driver swung into the traffic. Then he turned his head again. "I feel forced to tell you, señor, that the Diario is only across the street."

"I'm aware of that," Gould told him. "But I am a lazy man and dislike crossing streets. I prefer to add to the wealth of taxi drivers who do as they are told without asking questions."

The driver shrugged. Bart Gould leaned back against the seat. Reflectively he tested with a thumb the razorsharp blade of the knife. San Barrios had really changed since his last visit. Of that there wasn't much doubt.

Rubén de la Vega greeted Gould with a warm, enthusiastic abrazo. The newspaper editor was of the same age as Gould but there all outward similarities ended. De la Vega was short, with a rotund face, dark eyes lively behind glasses thickly rimmed with tortoise shell. He had the slightly oriental cast of features encountered so often in Central America.

He drew away from Gould, studied him for a moment with speculative amusement, then demanded, "What happened to the side of your face? Wouldn't you take no for an answer?"

Gould shrugged. "Some girl I've never seen before." "You are losing your technique, my friend."

"But not my sense of curiosity." Gould tossed the handbag and the knife onto the editor's desk. Briefly he recounted what had taken place during the curious encounter on the street.

"What do you make of it, Rubén?"

De la Vega frowned down at the display on his desk. He poked at the sharp blade of the knife with a neatly manicured forefinger. Then he picked up the handbag of lizard skin, regarded it thoughtfully, and murmured, "This is not a cheap item." He opened the clasp, upended the bag and dumped the contents out on his desk. He began separating the items with a finger, reciting the inventory as he went along. "A linen and lace handkerchief holding a fragrance with which I am not, unfortunately, familiar. A lipstick bearing the mark of Christian Dior. Expensive here, due to the heavy import tax on such luxuries. A powder compact of gold and enamel. A lottery ticket. A key ring with four keys. A thin billfold containing—let us see, 100, 100, 250, 285 pesos." He picked up the powder compact again, turning it over with sensitive fingers. "This is a choice little item. And there is engraving on the bottom. *To Paquita, 1961—R. G.* Paquita. That would be the diminutive for Francisca. R. G. might be anyone. It is something to think about."

Gould reached over, picked up the small handkerchief and held it to his nose. "For your information, Rubén, this is a jasmin fragrance put out by Chanel. Expensive even in Europe. It's not obtainable in the States."

De la Vega raised a mocking eyebrow. "You know so many interesting things, Bartolomé. The result of a classical education, no doubt." He continued studying the ornate compact with a faint frown. "Paquita. There is a girl of that name who displays a modest voice and an immodest amount of an excellent figure at the Flamingo, our leading attempt at a sophisticated nightclub. Do you think you might recognize her picture?"

"It is possible."

De la Vega reached for one of the phones on his desk, punched a button and spoke briefly and rapidly into the mouthpiece. Hanging up he turned back to Gould. "As I thought, we have a number of publicity photographs of the girl. We will have a look at them and then be on our way in time for an appropriate number of drinks before we eat."

Gould shook his head. "Not today, I'm afraid. I have an appointment at our embassy."

De la Vega glanced at him sharply. "Just a courtesy call, I presume?"

"Naturally. What else would it be."

The newspaper editor hesitated briefly. "I think you should know that I have a great deal of respect for Roger Hammet. He is the best man your country has sent down here in my recollection. Muy simpatico in every sense of the word. That is why I dislike seeing him get into trouble."

"He is in trouble?"

"Apparently. And don't ask me what it specifically is. I just don't know. It's one of those things you can't put a finger on. But anonymous stories and anonymous tips come in to us. Nothing definite—just the sort of vague innuendos that make a newspaper suspicious. And as a general rule when a newspaper gets suspicious any little thing can be exaggerated way out of proportion."

A short rap on the door interrupted him. An office boy came in, placed a large folder on his desk.

De la Vega dismissed the waiting boy with a gesture, opened the folder, flicked over the half a dozen glossy prints it contained.

Finally he selected one, slid it across the desk. "Does this ring any sort of a bell?"

Gould picked up the 8 by 10 print and studied it. It was a typical glamour publicity shot, showing a girl in a glittering sequin dress that seemed to have been painted on her body. The lighting had been arranged so as to emphasize the cleavage between the full mounds of her almost completely revealed breasts. The waist was small, the hips curved outward in the exaggeration of femininity that appeals to the average Latin American male.

Gould tossed the photo back on the desk with a faint sigh. "Unfortunately it was the face I saw and not quite so much of the figure. I can't say yes—but on the other hand, it could well enough be."

De la Vega laughed. "I hoped you would say that. Now we have an excellent reason for going out on the town tonight, starting at the Flamingo. There you can view this Paquita in the flesh, very much so, and reach a decision. Afterwards we shall see what we shall see."

"Remembering previous such excursions with you, that should be plenty," Gould told him. "Suppose I meet you at the Flamingo."

"Between nine-thirty and ten." De la Vega came around the desk and walked to the door with him. "Until then, tiene cuidado, hombre. I don't like the thought of losing a good drinking companion."

CHAPTER SIX

FROM THE moment he walked into the Embassy at exactly two minutes to one Bart Gould felt a curious air of uncertainty, as though the whole place were just marking time. There was only a small amount of activity to be seen. Gould glanced swiftly about the wide reception hall, noting the apparent absence of the Marine guards usually on duty at United States embassies throughout the world. Then he saw a stolid, square-jawed young man in a light blue drip-dry suit that he wore like a uniform hovering about the receptionist's desk, trying without success to look as though he just happened to be there on routine business.

The receptionist was a pale blonde girl of indefinite years who evidently took her position more seriously than her femininity. She was wearing a black tailored dress set off by white collar and cuffs, very little make-up and reading glasses that she took off when she looked up from the papers on her desk.

She studied Gould as he approached, mistook the deep tan on his face for a natural color, asked crisply, "Si, señor, puedo ayudarle?"

"It is a possibility," Gould said dryly. "At the moment I have an appointment. The name is Bartholomew Gould."

The carefully anonymous young man who was in the process of moving away from the desk turned sharply to stare at him. The receptionist lost some of her mannered efficiency. "I'm sorry, Mr. Gould, I didn't realize—"

"Quite all right," Gould told her. "Now if you'd just announce me."

"Yes, sir." She leaned forward to the intercom box on her desk, spoke into it. She glanced back at Gould. "You are expected. The office is just at the top of the stairs."

"I know. I've been here in the past."

He started up the wide curving staircase. Halfway up he paused, one hand on the polished rosewood balustrade, looking down into the wide foyer. He saw both the girl and the marine in mufti staring up at him. He said, "I think I sould tell you, soldier, that your gun is showing. Evenn though it's not regulations, I suggest a shoulder holster."

Roger Hammet was a tall, thin man in his late forties. He had slightly stooped shoulders and dark, greyish blue eyes that looked overstrained. His light brown hair refused to stay combed, always seemed in need of cutting.

He greeted Gould courteously but with an air of reserve. "I think we met once or twice in Washington."

"That's right. At luncheon at the Cosmos Club when you were a special guest."

"So it was." Hammet spoke with a faint air of regret, as though wishing for a return of those days when his interest in Latin American economics had been purely academic. "I had somehow expected to hear from you before this, Mr. Gould."

Gould frowned, wondering if Washington had changed its mind about advising Hammet of his mission. He said carefully, "So? Any particular reason, may I ask?"

"The usual one."

"And that is?"

Hammet leaned back, drawing a thumb and forefinger across his eyes. "Let's face facts, Mr. Gould. You have some very heavy investments in this country—investments that in the past have been extremely lucrative. These are now unsettled times. There are all sorts of rumors afloat here, including the usual one of expropriation. Why should you be any different than the others who come running to us demanding that something be done by our government to protect their property?"

"Because I don't believe in it," Gould said flatly. "I just don't happen to belong to that group that lambasts our government for doing too much for too many, while at the same time expecting the same government to come to my private aid. When I want Washington to go to bat to protect my income I'll invest in government bonds."

Hammet gave him a long, thoughtful stare. "I'm surprised to hear you say that, Mr. Gould. And, I might add, somewhat relieved."

"Nothing to be surprised at. However, I'm naturally interested in what is going on here. Any foundation to these rumors of political unrest?"

A long moment passed before the ambassador answered. "Frankly, I don't know. In politics, both domestic and international, it's not always true that where there is smoke there is fire. These days the smoke is too often synthetic. According to the best of information there is no strong communist group here. Castro hasn't been able to stir up many supporters. By our standards, old Hector Alvarez is pretty much of a dictator, but he hasn't the pathological greediness and sadistic mania for power that marked such men as Batista and Trujillo. He is neither feared nor hated by the masses. If you wanted to classify him I suppose you might call him a Salazar with more humane feelings and more of a sense of social consciousness." He broke off and drew his fingers over his eyes again. "No, I don't think Alvarez can be blamed directly or indirectly for the things that are now taking place."

"What sort of things?"

Hammet suddenly looked very tired. "I wish I knew the answer to that. All I can say is that it's a nightmarish situation." He made a marked effort to throw off his weariness. "But that's not your headache, Mr. Gould. I suggest we join my wife for a cocktail before luncheon. In that respect I still go against the native custom. I can't bring myself to face a heavy meal in the middle of the day."

Gould managed to conceal his feeling of surprise when he met Hammet's wife. Clare Hammet was at least fifteen years younger than her husband, at least as tall, a pale ash blonde with icy blue eyes and almost classic Nordic features. She was wearing a dress of thin seagreen material that emphasized her statuesque figure, a figure that she seemed aloofly unaware of. Yet when she moved her inner thighs seemed to caress one another as though engaged in some private sexual exercise of their own.

For the moment Gould reserved judgment.

He confined himself to casual social conversation while he sipped at an indifferent martini. Made, so his palate told him, of a local gin and probably a Mexican vermouth that was too sweet. Even when properly prepared, which was all too seldom, he didn't care for cocktails before a meal. He preferred a true aperitif, something tartly bitter like a dubonnet or a campari, to wet the appetite. Raw gin no matter how doctored simply deadened the taste buds.

At the luncheon table Clare Hammet's conversation took a probing turn. "You are down here from Washington, Mr. Gould?"

Gould swallowed a morsel of red snapper before answering. "That depends somewhat on what you mean. I have a home in Washington, but I'm afraid I'm not there very often."

"You mean that your work takes you away most of the time?"

"You compliment me. I'm afraid I haven't any real work, in the true meaning of the word. I'm what our friends, the communists, would call a capitalist drone."

"I can't quite believe that."

Gould wondered if her words were merely idle or if she somehow had an inkling of the true purpose of his visit. It could be that she was being no more than over-protective of her husband, suspicious now of every circumstance.

Gould changed the subject deliberately. "That was an unfortunate accident that happened to Drake."

Clare Hammet said quickly, "You know about that? I wasn't aware that the details had been made public."

Gould had a curious feeling of having inadvertently revealed knowledge he shouldn't have possessed. He said easily, "I heard about it from a classmate at the Princeton Club. A friend of the family."

"Oh? It was the chauffeur's fault, of course. He had been drinking."

"That's something I still don't understand." Hammet broke in. "Ortega was always very sober and conscientious."

"He drank," Clare Hammet said firmly. "More than once when he had occasion to drive me alone somewhere I detected liquor on his breath."

Hammet looked at her with a frown. "Why didn't you ever mention it to me?"

"I didn't want to add to your worries, Roger, dear. You have enough on your mind as it is. And he was never actually drunk in my presence. It was just that I smelled liquor. But I'm sure Mr. Gould isn't interested in problems that we no longer have."

To the contrary, Gould felt like saying, he was very much interested. He managed to keep his race expressionless.

Shortly the conversation turned to the upcoming O.A.S. conference due to open in just seven days. Roger Hammet was scheduled to make the opening address at the first meeting, immediately following the speech of welcome to the delegates by Hector Alvarez.

If nothing happened to upset those plans, Gould reminded himself. The threat to sabotage that conference, and discredit the United States, now seemed far less fantastic than it had in Titus Banning's office less than twenty-four hours before.

When Gould prepared to leave after the luncheon Hammet insisted that the embassy car drive him back to the hotel. Gould started to refuse and then thought better of it.

The driver of the embassy car was a thin, ascetic looking mestizo. He wasn't in uniform, but wore a white stetson hat, a white guayabera and neatly pressed almost white chinos.

As Gould settled himself on the rear seat in the new Chevrolet he remarked casually, "I take that you are the new chauffeur."

"Sí, señor. Enrique Aguilar, a sus órdenes."

Gould kept his tone casual. "I suppose you knew the unfortunate driver who had the job before you."

"Sí, señor. He was my cousin."

"A sad thing to happen, was it not? And sadder still that now they say that it happened while under the influence of strong drink. It is not right to defame a man who cannot any longer protect his reputation."

For a moment the driver concentrated on easing the car through the afternoon traffic. Then without turning his head he said, "It gives me great pain to say it, señor, but the stories are correct. Manuel was indeed a man who on occasion drank too heavily."

"It is a natural thing for a man to drink. It makes the accident no less unfortunate."

"Sí, señor."

A moment passed in silence. Then Gould suggested, "You say you are his cousin. Perhaps you can tell me where he lived."

"For what purpose, señor?"

Again Gould extemporized. "He was married, was he not? It is possible that his widow may need some aid. The family of Señor Drake, who died with him, requested that I attend to the matter."

Aguilar drove for a full block before answering. "That is quite thoughtful of them, señor. Manuel would have appreciated it. He lived in the Barrio of Magdalena, on the outskirts of the city. There is no street name, but anyone there could direct you to the house. You are thinking of going there this afternoon?"

"No. Today I have other matters to attend to. But possibly tomorrow."

"You should have no difficulty in finding the place. Perhaps if you speak to Mr. Hammet he would permit me to drive you there myself."

Gould thanked him but assured him it wouldn't be necessary. He lit a cigarette and puffed thoughtfully at it. Perhaps he was needlessly suspicious, but everyone seemed to be hiding something. He let his mind dwell momentarily on Clare Hammet.

For no good reason he thought of carnivorous plants that feed on insects.

Suddenly Gould changed his mind about going back to his hotel. He had less than an hour to kill before his appointment with the presidente. What he needed most, he now decided, was a strong drink and a quiet place to enjoy it in. He leaned forward, tapped the driver on the shoulder and gave directions for dropping him off at the St. Regis.

As the car circled the Plaza de Libertad, Gould's attention was caught by the spectacle of a group made up largely of young men, with a sprinkling of older, stolidfaced Indians, listening to a speaker perched on the high pedestal supporting the statue of Hector Alvarez.

Gould addressed the driver. “What goes on?”

“It is a person called Gómez. A Fidelista, so they say. He is protesting the proposed embargo on trade with Cuba and demanding a change in our government.”

“The police don’t bother him?”

The driver shrugged. “Our presidente is getting old. Perhaps he is no longer aware of certain things.”

Gould wondered.

CHAPTER SEVEN

HECTOR ALVAREZ, the presidente of San Barrios, could easily have passed for a retired master-sergeant, which was exactly what he had been when the United States Marines occupied the country some three decades before. He was in his late sixties, of medium height with a stocky build. Despite a slight paunch he still retained a military bearing, even in the dark blue double-breasted suit he affected. His skin was pale olive in color, marked by liver spots.

He greeted Gould with a warm familiarity, rising from behind his desk to give him an abrazo. "Don Bartolomé. Qué milagro!"

Gould responded to the greeting in kind. As he made himself comfortable in the deep leather chair towards which Alvarez waved him he noted that the president looked older than he had expected, far older than the intervening three years since he had last seen him would normally warrant.

"What brings you back to our country?"

It was a question Gould had expected and he had his answer ready. "It's been a long time since my last visit. I don't believe in being an absentee landlord. And then there is the upcoming conference of the O.A.S. I thought that might be interesting to observe at close hand."

Old Alvarez eyed him shrewdly. "No other reason? Not, let us say, because of any rumors you might have heard in Washington?"

Gould managed a laugh. "I'll tell you the same thing I said during luncheon at the embassy earlier. I just happen to have a house in Washington. But I pay little attention to politics."

Alvarez smiled patiently, shaking his head slowly. "Others might believe that, my dear Bartolomé, but I do not. You may be a playboy, and muy macho with the ladies, but you are not a fool. So you had luncheon with your ambassador? How did Mr. Hammet seem to you?"

Gould considered his answer carefully. "He seemed to have a great deal on his mind."

"That I can well imagine. He made no mention of the things that were worrying him?"

"Not at all."

The president of San Barrios sighed. "I don't suppose he would. But you noticed something. And you must have noticed, too, that the atmosphere of our country here is not exactly without tension."

"That is true of most of the Latin American countries right now, isn't it?"

"Unfortunately, yes. We have always had communist groups which we managed, when left alone, to handle in our own way. Now the Fidelistas are taking advantage of outside pressures. If we follow the United States lead too strongly, we are accused of being puppets of the yanqui imperialists. We are being ground between the two extremes. And there are men clever enough to take advantage of our dilemma."

Gould mentioned the speaker he had seen at the Plaza de Libertad on his way to the palace. Alvarez nodded. "That would be Ramón Gómez. A calculated risk. He has been a political firebrand since his days at the university. But it has been mostly wild talk of the kind all young men engage in. Up until recently he had no followers and no financial backing."

"And now he has?"

"The money, yes, although for the moment not too many followers. The usual students and riff-raff. We are trying to discover where his backing comes from. Our first suspicion, naturally, was that it was Soviet money. But that doesn't seem likely. Gómez rants against Russia as much as he does against me. Actually, he doesn't seem to have much of a program. He is simply against everything."

"Sounds as though he belongs to one of our right-wing groups at home," Gould suggested. "So for the time being you let him run loose?"

"I didn't say that. We keep him under close observation." Again Alvarez sighed heavily. "I will be glad when this conference is over with and the world spotlight is no longer on this little country. Then perhaps we can handle certain things a bit more firmly." He reached out and pressed a button on the side of his desk. "But I'm forgetting my manners, Bartolomé. We should have a copita to celebrate your return. I trust it will be a pleasant visit. But I regret sincerely that I must tell you to watch yourself. These are unsettled times."

It was six thirty when he left the presidential palace. An official car drove him back to the Palace Hotel. Getting out of the car, Gould stood for a moment on the sidewalk talking to the driver, a young man in an army uniform of french blue that denoted his attachment to the president's palace guard.

As he stood talking to the driver, Gould studied the street with more attention than he normally would have given. He noticed a big, dusty sedan parked diagonally across the avenue. His attention was momentarily diverted by the fact that despite the nondescript appearance of the massive car he recognized it as an old Daimler, a model famous for its reserve of power and stamina. The driver, an equally nondescript appearing mestizo, lounged behind the wheel, looking neither to right nor left. As Gould watched, he was startled by the appearance of a strange figure emerging from a nearby tobacco shop and approaching the car. A grotesquely short, grotesquely ugly man with the torso of a giant wrestler attached to the short, bowed legs of a dwarf. The monstrosity approached the dusty Daimler, was lost to sight for a moment before he slid onto the seat beside the driver. A second later, with a throaty roar of its powerful motor, the car shot smoothly away.

Gould eyed the young officer who had driven him from the presidential palace. "That's something you don't see very often."

"No, señor."

"Did you recognize the car by any chance?"

"No, señor. Only the enano. He works for one señor Norden, who has a large finca on the other side of the lake."

"Interesting," Gould said. "Thanks again for driving me."

Gould turned and walked into the lobby of the hotel. He stopped at the desk for his room key. Sánchez, the middle-aged room clerk who had been on duty that morning, had been replaced by a younger man. A plaque on the registration counter announced that his name was Roberto Frías. He handed Gould his key and a slip of paper. "A señor Wagner has been trying to reach you several times during the late afternoon. Both by telephone and in person."

Gould thanked him and crossed the lobby towards the wide stairway leading to the balconies of the second floor. He wondered just how his estate manager had discovered so quickly that he was in the country.

It was one of a number of other puzzling things that needed an answer.

Despite the sultry heat outside, his rooms were comfortably cool because of the thick walls and high ceilings. He walked over to the phone, asked for room service, and ordered a bottle of ron negrito. Then he checked his cigarette supply, noticed he was running short, and picking up the phone again ordered a dozen packages of Casinos, a cigarette made locally out of rich tobacco leaf grown in the valley of the rio Dulce. He took off his jacket and tie, unbuttoned his shirt collar.

When room service arrived he signed the check and dug into his pocket for a tip. He poured himself a stiff drink of the dark rum, ignoring the bucket of ice cubes. Then he lit a cigarette and sprawled in the one easy chair the living room afforded.

Thoughtfully he considered the day's happenings since stepping off the plane at the airport that morning.

On the surface there seemed to be only disconnected loose ends, but Gould had a strong hunch those loose ends were all connected at some hidden point.

One thing seemed certain. His sudden visit to San Barrios was attracting more than normal attention. Why this should be he didn't know. Possibly it might have some connection with the threats made against Hammet and the United Sates but that was just jumping at the easiest conclusion.

Now the sensible thing to do was rest while he could, waiting for the next move of the unseen forces at play.

He finished the remainder of his rum, snubbed out his cigarette, went into the bedroom and stretched out for a needed nap.

CHAPTER EIGHT

AT NINE FORTY-FIVE that evening Bart Gould paid off his taxi, crossed the sidewalk, walked into the outer foyer of the Flamingo. To the right was the checkroom attended by two young girls in adaptations of the traditional Indian costumes of San Barrios, with colorfully embroidered blouses of thin cambaya cut revealingly low. To the left was the entrance to the bar. Straight ahead solid swinging doors covered with gold leaf, each decorated with a bas relief of a pink flamingo, led into the night club itself.

Gould found De la Vega waiting for him in the bar, nursing a Scoth and soda and talking to a man whom he introduced as the O.A.S. delegate from Colombia. "We were, believe it or not, not discussing what to do about Castro."

"I'll take your word for it."

"You sound disbelieving, but I assure you it is true. Instead we were discussing what to do about the Dominican Republic if the military attempts another coup."

Gould nodded and glanced around the bar as he listened to the Colombian expounding the psychological reasons for and against a policy of non-intervention. At each end of the bar there was a man drinking alone, each looking slightly out of place.

Their elaborate efforts at nonchalance marked them as secret police agents.

At the Colombian's insistence Gould took a highball of rum and water. "You are here for the conference, señor Gould?"

Gould shook his head. "No. I just happen to be passing through." He was aware of De la Vega giving him a sharp glance and he smiled blandly as he placed a hand on his shoulder. "My friend here has promised to show me the night life of the town."

There was another moment or two of conversation before they left the Colombian delegate in the bar and moved on into the main room of the night club. It was already crowded, but De la Vega had previously reserved a table on the rim of the dance floor. The headwaiter, an Italian, made a production of seeing them to their places, hovering over the table until De la Vega ordered drinks and sent him on his way. "We'll decide what we want to eat later."

Then the newspaper editor squinted thoughtfully through his glasses. "And just what, manito, is the point of putting on the visiting stranger act?"

Bart Gould smiled. "Why not? As I have already been reminded by unimpeachable sources, San Barrios has changed considerably since last I was here. That makes me something of a stranger, doesn't it?"

"Tú dices. As a newspaper man may I ask about your unimpeachable sources?"

"You may. I had already reached that conclusion for myself before I was reminded of the fact at the Palace this afternoon."

"You mean old Alvarez admitted as much?"

Gould nodded.

"I didn't think he was that well aware of what is going on," De la Vega half grunted. He picked up the elaborate, oversized menu, glanced briefly at it, and put it to one side. "No sense in studying this thing. Half of the things on it they don't have but I can highly recommend the grilled shrimp to start with and then pavita parrillada. They have an excellent chef here and that particular dish is his specialty. I can promise you it will be a treat even for your jaded palate."

"I'm sure it will," Gould said. "I take it that the chef is from the Argentine."

De la Vega paused in the process of lighting a cigarette. "Now how the hell did you guess that?"

Gould laughed. "Simple deduction. The pavita parrillada gave it away. The last time I enjoyed it was at the Jockey Club in Buenos Aires, where it originated." He half closed his eyes, remembering with anticipatory pleasure. As though talking to himself, he murmured, "Baby turkeys, split in half and marinated for a sufficient time in a medium sweet white wine,—personally I prefer a barsac—mixed with sufficient lemon juice to counteract the sweetness and given distinction with a light touch of freshly made garlic salt, newly ground black pepper and a few pinches of rosemary. Then brushed with a sauce made up of pure Spanish olive oil, properly seasoned with salt, black pepper, crushed rosemary, salsa inglesa, wine vinegar and a mild mustard. Grilled over hot coals until they are a rich ruddy color. Placed in a serving dish, with warm brandy poured over them and served flambé. You are quite correct when you say it will stimulate my jaded palate."

De la Vega gave a mock sigh. "I should have known better than to try to impress you. Just for knowing so damned much I'll let you select the wines."

"Why not. A white burgundy with the shrimp and a light red for the pavitas. Pommard '49 if they have it." Gould grinned at his old friend cheerfully, then he leaned back in his chair and sent a slow glance around the room. The Flamingo had the appearance of a typical Latin American night club. Narrow balconies placed high up on the walls, supported by tall arches, gave the room the illusion of being an outdoor patio. On one side of the room, at the far end of the small dance floor, there was a raised bandstand. There were two orchestras, one a Latin version of a Dixieland Jazz band with an overemphasis on brass, the other a Guatemalan marimba group.

"There's not too much here by way of entertainment," De la Vega said. "But what we lack in quality we make up in noise. There is a flamenco group that comes on first but I advise you not to expect too much. The girl is handsome enough but far from being any Carmen Amaya. Her talents lie in other directions, according to some of my more lecherous friends. As might be said for the young lady we have come to see."

Gould nodded. He was still busy trying to adjust himself to the changed atmosphere of the country. He glanced around the crowded room again, mentally trying to ticket the diners. In the past San Barrios had always been a quiet, almost feudal country, with little of the garish night life that characterizes more modern countries. When men went out in the evening they went either to their club or a cafe. It had never been a country that attracted tourists in any large numbers and so had not had to cater to their entertainment.

Now he asked, "Is it as crowded as this every night?"

"Not quite. Don't forget that the town is filled with delegates and their staffs for the conference. But usually there is a fairly good crowd nevertheless. Why?"

"It's not like the San Barrios I knew."

"You remarked before that it had changed. So has all the rest of the world, my friend. Fiddling while Rome burns and all the rest."

There was a sudden loud fanfare from the orchestra, the lights dimmed, a spot picked out the master of ceremonies standing at a microphone at the edge of the bandstand.

"Y ahora, damas y caballeros, el grupo de Flamenco más famoso directamente de Andalucía."

The orchestra, the brasses muted and augmented now by two guitars, picked up the rhythm. There was a click of castanets. Gould glanced toward the circle of light on the dance floor long enough to discover that the girl going into the opening movements of Alegrías was wearing form-fitting slacks, a recent innovation of flamenco dancers of which he strongly disapproved. For his money something was lost in the sensuous, fiery movements of the true flamenco when the traditional skirt, tight from hip to knee and flaring out in a ruffled train, was discarded.

He turned his attention to the grilled shrimp. In a break between numbers De la Vega said casually, "How was your session with your Ambassador?"

"Routine." Gould paused to test the Corton Charlemange. As always when he savoured this particular burgundy he thought of the Chardonnay grapes, big and golden in color, which produced it. It was harder and more steely to the taste than the softer, more popular white wines, but he much preferred it. Moreover, unlike the majority of white wines, it had the added virtue of lasting through the years without diminishing in quality. He moved the glass slowly under his nose, seeing if he could detect the faint perfume of cinnamon that so many connoisseurs insisted was present. He was never quite sure whether he really did detect it or it was just his preconditioned imagination at work. "Simply routine," he repeated. "Merely the usual courtesy call."

"Still being cagey? I've never known you to be quite, so discreet, Bartolomé. It gives one to wonder."

Gould said lightly. "Good mental exercise for a newspaper man. Particularly for an editor who is becoming too fat and pampered with soft living."

De la Vega grunted. "You sure as hell can't mean me. You had luncheon at the Embassy so you must have met Hammet's famously beautiful wife. What did you think of her?"

Again Gould hesitated slightly before answering. "She is pleasant to look at." Then a thought struck him. "Tell me something. How did your newspaper handle the story of Hobart Drake's death?"

This time it was De la Vega who made a marked pause. "Why do you ask?"

"Does there have to be any particular reason?"

"In this case, yes. Because there are two answers to your question. As to how my paper handled the story, in print we simply confined ourselves to a brief account of the tragic accident. We followed it up with an editorial demanding that stronger safety rails be put on the mountain curves."

"And the other answer?"

"The other answer is what makes running a newspaper so damned frustrating. The chauffeur, Ortega, as you probably have heard, was supposed to be drunk at the time. I sent some of my best reporters out on the story and they came back with some highly conflicting accounts. I was just getting ready to blow the whole thing up into the kind of mystery that builds circulation when I received a polite but pointed suggestion from on high that it would be just as well to drop the whole matter. Business of not creating a diplomatic incident and all the rest." De la Vega broke off to applaud perfunctorily the end of a number, then turned his attention back to Gould. "So you can see now why I am curious that you should ask about it."

Gould remained silent for a moment, wondering just how much he should tell his old friend. Then he reminded himself that he was on a lone wolf assignment where the normal standards of friendship didn't count. He said finally, "Put it down for the moment that I'm just inquiring as a friend of the family."

The Flamenco group finished, the sound of the staccato rhythms was momentarily replaced by the rising hum of voices and clatter of silverware. Then another brief musical introduction brought back the master of ceremonies.

"Y ahora, damas y caballeros, la guapa cantante Paquita ofreciéndoles las canciones más modernas de Europa."

There was a round of applause led, so Gould noticed with wry amusement, by the waiters. The spotlight changed from bright amber to a pale rose. The girl Paquita moved from the shadows on the far side of the bandstand into the spot.

She was wearing a dramatically revealing evening gown of sleak white satin that accentuated the slightly tawny tones of her skin. In one hand she carried an oversized black handerchief of sheer chiffon and lace—the Hildegard influence, Gould decided wearily.

Paquita sent a professional smile at the unseen faces in the darkened room. "Mi primer número, la canción favorita actualmente, *Nunca en Domingo*."

From the piano in the background came the first chords of *Never on Sunday.*

De la Vega leaned across the table. "How about it. Is she the one?"

Gould nodded slowly. "I'm pretty sure. She looks like it and sounds like it."

"There is one way of making it certain," De la Vega said. "We'll send for her to come to our table after she's finished her turn. And if she is the one it will give you a chance to find out what was behind her little act this morning."

"I have a feeling that it won't be that easy."

"But it should be interesting." De la Vega extracted a card from his wallet, scribbled on the back of it, then beckoned a passing captain of the waiters and instructed him to see that it was handed to the singer the moment she came off the floor. "Of course, there's always the chance that she may take another swing at you. But I'm here to protect you this time."

Without emphasis Gould told him what he could do with his protection. He listened with half an ear to the girl while she went through the stock numbers always heard in any Latin American night club, with the emphasis mostly on the compositions of Agustin Lara. There was *Solamente Una Vez,* followed by *María Bonita,* and then *Señora Tentación.* Finally, as Gould had subconsciously expected, she switched continents for her final number, *La Vida en Rosa.*

She bowed off at last, the room lights came back on, the final faint waves of applause were swallowed up in the sound of the marimbas beginning the *Song of Tehuantepec.*

Without making a point of it Gould watched through narrowed eyes as the singer moved around the edge of the bandstand towards the curtained archway leading to the dressing rooms. He saw the captain of the waiters stop her, hand her De la Vega's card, then gesture towards their table.

She turned, threading her way around the dancers now filling the floor. "The power of the press," De la Vega murmured. "No entertainer, particularly a woman, is going to lose the chance of getting some publicity."

Gould didn't answer. He was intent on watching the girl as she neared the table. He saw her stop suddenly, eyes widening in startled apprehension. Quickly Gould bent his head, trying to mask his face with the business of lighting a cigarette.

It was too late.

When he looked again the girl was gone. He half arose from his chair, trying to catch a glimpse of her over the heads of the dancers. He thought he saw her disappearing through an arched doorway on the far side of the room but couldn't be sure.

Watching him, De la Vega demanded, "What now?"

"The girl. For once the attraction of free publicity isn't enough. She caught one glimpse of me and took off."

De la Vega was on his feet. "Come along. We'll corner her in her dressing room."

Gould followed the editor as he circled his way through the tables. They cut across a corner of the dance floor, held up momentarily by the crush of dancers. They reached the curtained archway at the far side of the bandstand. De la Vega pushed through and turned to the left. A short flight of stairs led down to the basement. One of the male Flamenco dancers was lounging in an open door way. Beyond him Gould caught a glimpse of the star of the group, sitting at her dressing table, munching on a chicken leg. A soiled dressing gown of once yellow silk hung negligently open, revealing the thin muscularity of her naked body. Her sloe eyes, holding the combination of insolence and speculation that marks the gypsy strain, flickered deliberately over Gould.

De la Vega addressed the lounging man. "El cuarto de Paquita?"

The man indicated the door of the room facing him. "Ahí, pero no está. Todavía está arriba."

"We'll wait then," De la Vega decided. He turned, put his hand on the knob, started to swing open the dressing room door.

"Un momento," the Flamenco dancer protested. "I have just said that Paquita is not down yet."

De la Vega gave him an impatient glance. "Do not molest yourself. We have an appointment of importance with the señorita."

They stepped inside the dressing room.

The room was small, barely large enough for a dressing table, a washstand and a couple of straight chairs. Stockings and a ruffled petticoat were draped over the top of a screen in one corner. Gould noticed the same scent of jasmin perfume that he had identified earlier on the handkerchief found in the handbag.

Gould said suddenly, "It may be that our little song bird has flown off without bothering to come down here. Suppose you go up above and make inquiries."

De la Vega nodded and turned on his heel.

Left alone in the room, Bart Gould paced restlessly, two strides in one direction, three in another. He paused by the dressing table, aimlessly fingering the pots of cream and makeup. A book on one end of the dressing table caught his eye and he picked it up. It was one of the popular works of Juan José Arévalo, the former Guatemalan president who had made a career out of baiting the United Fruit Company's activities in his country. That figured. He opened the book. There was a name written on the fly leaf. Ramón Gómez.

That would be the R. G. whose initials were on the gold powder compact. And, quite possibly, it was the same Ramón Gómez he had seen haranguing a crowd from the pedestal of the President's statue in the Plaza de Libertad that afternoon.

That much tied up. What wasn't clear was the reason behind the abortive attack on him earlier. Granted that the rabble-rouser might be rabidly anti-American, sufficiently so as to provoke an attack on him. But the timing was wrong. It had come too quickly after his arrival, at the time when his presence in the country was known only to a few people.

He was still trying to fit the business into some logical pattern when De la Vega returned. The newspaper editor spread his hands outward, palms upward, in a gesture of failure.

"No luck. According to the doorman she went flying out of the place as though the devil himself were after her. She jumped into a passing taxi and took off."

"Can you find out where does she lives?"

"I already thought of that. Mario, the manager here, claims he doesn't know. The address she gave when she first came to work here was one of the small hotels nearby but she has moved since. I can find out—one of my police reporters can ferret out anything, including the truth from a politico—but it will take time."

"How long?"

De la Vega shrugged. "A few hours. Possibly less. But I'll have to go back to the paper to start the wheels spinning. Want to come with me?"

Gould hesitated, then shook his head. "I think I'll turn in. It looks as though I'm going to have a long day tomorrow and I want to do a little advance planning."

"Then I'll telephone you the information as soon as I get it."

"Do that," Gould said. Then he had a sudden second thought. "I'd appreciate if you sent the information around by messenger instead of telephoning."

De la Vega gave him a sharp look. "Becoming suspicious of everything, aren't you? I've a feeling there is more to this than you're telling me. Anything else I can do for you?"

Gould said slowly, "Now that you mentioned it, there is. I came down here a little unprepared for the sort of welcome I'm receiving and haven't had a chance as yet to get out to my finca and properly outfit myself. Until I do, I'd appreciate the loan of an automatic—a small Luger will do, if you have one—and one of your cars. As I remember, you used to have an old Cord that you kept in good shape."

De la Vega seemed to find the request natural. His only reaction was to raise one eyebrow. "I still do keep it in good shape. Fortunately one of our second-rate matadors had one years ago and managed to smash it up the second time he was behind the wheel. I bought the wreck so that I still have replacement parts available. I'll send it around to the hotel along with the gun."

They had moved back upstairs into the nightclub. They paused at their table only long enough to settle the check. Gould glanced down regretfully at the cold, by now inedible portion of pavita parrillada.

Outside the club De la Vega offered to drive him back to the hotel before returning to his newspaper. Gould decided against it. "I'll walk," he said. "I'm still trying to find out just what has changed the feeling of this place."

De la Vega gave a brief laugh that was strangely without his customary overtones of humor. "You're not alone in looking for the answer. Bueno, hasta pronto."

"Until tomorrow," Gould said. He stood on the sidewalk until De la Vega had flagged down a cab and stepped into it. Then he turned and started slowly in the direction of the hotel.

The Flamingo was on a sidestreet, just two blocks off the Avenida Colón. Instead of heading back to that principle thoroughfare, Gould decided to go along the 5 de Marzo that ran parallel to it. The 5 de Marzo was less modern, more typical of the country. For a half dozen blocks it was lined with small cantinas, boticas, all-night restaurants, and movie houses advertising ancient American and Mexican films. He paused to glance at a lobby display of Cantinflas in El Bolero de Raquel and recalled with a touch of pleasant nostalgia the wife of the Scandinavian Ambassador with whom he had seen the film in Mexico City some five years before. And he recalled other, even pleasanter, moments he had spent with her.

He moved on along the street. Gradually the lighted shop fronts and the crowds along the sidewalks thined. In the last half dozen blocks before 5 de Marzo crossed the Avenida Santiago only an occasional cantina spilled light and sound into the street.

Then, subconsciously at first, Gould became aware of a slight change in the pattern of the figures moving along the street. On the opposite side he noted a half dozen shadowy figures moving abreast of him, separate but all headed in the same direction. A dark sedan passed him moving slowly. He caught a glimpse of steel helmets. He saw the car slow to stop a block ahead of him and a half dozen uniformed men pile out.

Bart Gould slowed his steps, warned by a feeling that there was something out of focus in the picture.

Instinctively he glanced back over his shoulder. Behind him there was only a scattering of pedestrians. He looked forward again. As if on a cue the men on the opposite side of the street who had been moving abreast of him now collected in a group on the corner half a block away, directly opposite the uniformed men. Then, as though still following orders from some unseen director, the two groups merged. There were shouts and cries, and then the shooting started.

Automatically Gould moved flat against the front of the building he was passing. He heard the whine of a bullet as it ricocheted off the stone facade inches from his head. Then flame seared his left shoulder and he flung himself face down on the ground, rolling over towards the meager shelter of a shallow doorway.

He heard a motor roar by and the sound of a more concentrated gun fire. He raised his head slightly. Another car load of soldiers had pulled up and was spilling out on the street. The crowd on the corner was disintegrating, vanishing more rapidly than it had gathered.

Gould raised himself up and still hugging the wall retraced his steps. He reached the corner, turned it quickly, and headed swiftly for the bright lights of Avenida Colón and a taxi.

He put a hand under his jacket and felt his shoulder. His fingers came away sticky with blood. It was nothing more serious than a flesh wound, he decided.

But that was quite enough for one evening.

The last thing before going to bed Gould left orders for his breakfast to be sent up at seven-thirty promptly.

He had just settled down to his first cup of coffee when a knock came on the door. It was a young man who identified himself as De la Vega's chauffeur. He handed Gould a small package, a note, and a set of car keys, with the information that the car was parked at one side of the hotel.

When he had gone Gould opened the package. It contained the Luger he had asked for, together with a shoulder holster. He examined the gun quickly, made sure it held a full clip and then dropped it into his dressing gown pocket. He opened the note, scanning the message De la Vega had written: *Our elusive friend lives presently in a small apartment house at number 16 Calle Leopoldo. The apartment, under the name of Montes, is 8A. Would you like me to go with you?*

Brief moments later Gould was again interrupted at his breakfast. This time it was an older man in army uniform. He introduced himself with stiff formality as Colonel Rodríguez.

"It is about last night, Señor Gould," he said after he had accepted a chair and declined coffee. "It was most unfortunate."

Gould said carefully, "It might have been worse."

"Indeed, yes. But it was also most puzzling."

Gould eyed him thoughtfully. "In what way?"

The colonel leaned forward. "Let me see if I have it correctly. You were very nearly killed by what was apparently a stray bullet fired by one of our federal police engaged in breaking up a small demonstration. Is that not so?"

"You seem very well informed."

"That is our business, Señor Gould. But what makes it puzzling is that no federal police were involved. Our men, most fortunately for you, arrived on the scene in time to break up the affair. The men who were masquerading in uniform fled along with the others."

Gould took a long moment to light a cigarette. "I see."

"Do you?" Colonel Rodríguez asked. "If so, it is more than I do. Have you any explanation as to why somebody should go to such lengths to murder you and make it appear a stupid accident caused by our government police?"

Gould thought swiftly, carefully keeping his face expressionless. Finally he shrugged in apparent perplexity. "Are you quite sure it wasn't just an accident or a case of my being mistaken for someone else? I can think of no other explanation."

Colonel Rodríguez looked at him searchingly, then sighed heavily as he rose to his feet. "I trust sincerely that you are correct, Señor Gould. Our President is much concerned and it would not go well with us who are in charge of security measures if next time such an accident succeeded in its purpose. You are sure there is no further information you can give?"

"Quite sure," Gould told him, and wondered if in so saying he was signing his own death warrant.

CHAPTER NINE

WHEN THE colonel left Gould picked up the phone, called room service and ordered the remains of his cold breakfast taken away and a fresh pot of black coffee sent up. He went into the bathroom and examined the flesh wound on his shoulder in the mirror over the washstand. It had been superficial, indicated now by scarcely more than the long brown stain of iodine with which he had smeared it before going to bed. He shaved and dressed, mentally planning the day ahead.

A knock came on the door and he opened it to find not only room service but Guillermo Wagner, the manager of his local holdings.

Wagner was a man in his early forties, of medium height with a stocky figure that he held stiffly erect as though standing at attention on some parade ground. He had been born in the country, his father a German engineer who had worked for Gould's uncle, his mother a native woman. Bart Gould had always taken him pretty much for granted, satisfied that he knew his business and did it well.

He usually left him to himself, making only occasional suggestions about the management of his estates. Wagner seemed to prefer it that way.

After a correctly formal greeting Wagner said, "I came early so as not to miss you. I was here several times yesterday but without success."

"So I understand." Gould gave him a quick, searching glance. "Why the hurry? Is there anything wrong at the finca?"

"No. Everything goes most splendidly. It is just that it seemed of importance that I make my report to you as soon as possible."

"I see." Gould lit a cigarette, trying to decide just what was different in the man's manner. Usually Wagner spoke and acted with a Teutonic crispness. But now there was an undertone of nervous uncertainty. Gould said laconically, "If that is so any report could have waited, could it not, until I came out to the finca?"

"I wished to save you the trip. Besides, there is a matter that needs your immediate decision."

"So? What is it?"

Wagner drew a deep breath and then started talking quickly. He reminded Gould that he had been away from the country for several years, that the political temper had changed and the future was now uncertain, that there were rumors of expropriation in the air. Particularly the expropriation of land owned by foreigners. At any moment such a thing might happen.

Gould listened with a faint frown. Finally he broke in, "All that I am aware of. Is this the matter of importance you couldn't wait to tell me?"

"No. I am here to inform you that there is a way out that will not involve any real loss on your part."

The frown still creasing his forehead, Gould said, "I'm listening."

"There is a person who will buy your properties, Señor Gould. Moreover, this person will pay a fair price."

Gould stared down at his manager for a long moment while he turned over the information in his mind. "This person," he said finally, "must be a native of the country if he does not fear expropriation."

Wagner hesitated. "He has the papers of a citizen."

"And his name?"

"I am not at liberty to tell you until I am assured that you are willing to sell. But I promise you there will be no difficulty over the money. It will be paid immediately."

"An interesting suggestion," Gould said noncommitally. "Something to think over."

Wagner said quickly, "But this is the point, Señor Gould. There is no time to think the offer over. It must be decided within the next day or so. Forty-eight hours at the most."

With slow deliberation Gould snubbed out the end of his cigarette and took a fresh one from the package on the table. Slowly he lit it, studying through narrowed eyes the first puff of smoke. Slowly he shook his head. "Not today, Wagner."

"But it is a most excellent offer. And when you consider the times—"

"I am considering the times," Gould broke in. "And if some unknown person can gamble on the value of my property so can I."

"But can I at least say that you will think it over?"

"You may not!" Gould said shortly. He continued staring thoughtfully at his manager. "And before we close the subject I find your eagerness for the sale a bit difficult to understand."

"I'm only thinking of your own interests, Señor Gould."

"I'm sure." For the first time Gould was aware of an active lack of liking for his employee. He glanced pointedly at his wrist watch. "Now, if there is nothing more, I have several engagements this morning."

"Nothing more, Señor Gould. But I fear you are going to regret your decision."

"That will be my worry."

After the man had gone Gould stood motionless in the center of the room, trying to fit this new bit into the puzzle that already confronted him. Finally he walked over to the telephone, picked it up and asked to be connected with the Diario de Colima. When finally he had De la Vega on the wire he exchanged morning greetings, thanked him for the items he had sent over, and then made a further request. "You have a detailed map of the country handy? Fine. Can you tell me if any one person owns or controls extensive property near my holdings on the western boundaries of the lake?" Gould held the phone, staring at the blank wall facing him while he tried to picture in his mind's eye the topography of the country.

De la Vega came back on the wire. "A man by the name of Kurt Norden owns the hacienda adjoining yours. A matter of some ten thousand hectareas."

"Who's he?"

"That's a good question, my friend. By all accounts he is a European financier who retired. Keeps to himself. He isn't seen much around Colima. And the reason for asking?"

"I just like to know my neighbors," Gould told him and hung up.

The name Norden nagged at his mind. Then he remembered where he had heard it last. According to the young officer who had driven him back to the hotel yesterday from the President's Palace that was the name of the owner of the big Daimler he had seen parked across the Avenue. The one the misshapen monstrosity of a dwarf had entered.

Had it been simply coincidence that the car happened to be there at just that time? Or had it been waiting for his return? And why should Norden be at all interested in his comings and goings?

He wondered, further, if the two abortive attempts on his life had been actual attempts to kill him or were simply efforts to frighten him away. Somebody seemed definitely not to want him in San Barrios. Why? If his true mission were the secret it was supposed to be, then it just didn't make any sense. He had no enemies in the country that he knew of. To the best of his knowledge there had never been any troubles on his estates. He wasn't even closely identified with them. Unlike the big fruit and mining companies he couldn't be singled out as a whipping boy by the anti-imperialists. Granted that there were elements in the country that now were intent on stirring up as much trouble as possible on the eve of the O.A.S. conference it was still too much of a coincidence that he had been so quickly picked on.

For the moment his mind dismissed the possibilities that there had been a leak in Washington.

Thoughtfully, frowning over his cigarette, he began to explore other possibilities. He tried to picture the mentality of the person behind the threats that had brought him to the country. A man with power, obviously, and with ruthless imagination. A man quick to suspect any possible obstacles to his diabolical scheming and equally quick to remove those obstacles, as witness the death of Hobart Drake on his way to catch the plane that would carry him to Washington. Just how much information had Drake possessed? Even more to the point, where and how had Drake obtained that information?

Drake, by all accounts, has been an overly-meticulous type who spent little time away from the Embassy. That left only one answer to the question.

The leak must be somewhere in the Embassy.

That, for the moment, was outside his province. The leak was important—but far more important was the discovery of the person to whom the information had been channeled. To find that person was now the most pressing problem. There wasn't time to do it secretly. There wasn't time, and there weren't any tangible clues. Now, with every hour counting, he could only use a technique that he had utilized before on big game hunts in Africa. Turn himself from the hunter into the hunted.

He had the feeling that wouldn't be too difficult. Obviously his presence in San Barrios was already suspect, that much was clear.

The moment he had made up his mind Gould was conscious of a sharp change in his mood. It was like the difference between planning for a safari, and actually starting out on one. When that moment occurred the familiar landscape at which you had looked for days with mild interest suddenly acquired a different, an almost living personality. For now each innocent clump of trees, each fold in the veldt, held potential danger. A sound, a movement that would have passed unnoticed before now acquired sudden significance. Danger was not alone where you found it—too often it sought you out where you stood waiting.

He glanced at his watch. It was now sixteen minutes past ten. The time for idle speculation, for regarding the whole business as an intriguing mental exercise, was over.

So was the time for moving in secrecy. From now on the more people who suspected his mission, the better.

First things first, he decided. That meant a call on the girl Paquita. He took the shoulder holster out of its wrapping, slipped it on and adjusted it. He inserted the Luger, and put on his jacket. The gun didn't make too much of a bulge. He picked up the keys to the Cord and put them into his pocket. Then he went over to his suitcase, unlocked it, and took out the lizard skin handbag and the knife that were the memento's of yesterday's curious business. He hesitated a moment, then put the knife in his inner jacket pocket, the sharp blade protected by the folds of his wallet.

CHAPTER TEN

OUTSIDE THE hotel he paused for a moment of indecision. He was tempted to try out De la Vega's old Cord. Then decided against it.

As he waited for a taxi he found himself glancing up and down the avenue, studying the parked cars, wondering if any were waiting to follow him. He looked particularly for the big Daimler but didn't see it.

Calle Leopoldo was in the old section of the city, halfway between the zocalo and the market place. Here were none of the gestures toward moderninity that marked the newer district around the avenidas Colón and Santiago. The buildings were old, the narrow sidewalks crowded with outdoor stands.

No. 16 was in the middle of a block, its entrance nearly hidden between a peluquería and a meat market. In contrast to the sharp morning brightness flooding the congested street, the small entrance hall was dark, gloomy, heavy with the odors of garlic and rancid cooking oil.

Gould took out his pocket lighter, flicked it on, looked about for the tenant directory. There was none. Instead one wall held a number of battered mail boxes, of varying sizes and shapes. He found one holding a card with the name MONTES printed on it in pencil. The card looked new.

The door leading from the entrance foyer pushed open to his touch. He walked in and started climbing the stairs. From the open doorway of one of the apartments came the sound of a radio, turned up to its top decibel of sound, with a falsetto tenor singing.

The building was three stories high. Apartment 8A was on the top floor. There was no name on the door and Gould stood in front of it for brief moments, considering.

Then he rapped sharply.

There was no immediate answer. He raised his hand to knock again and stopped when he heard movement on the other side of the door.

A girl's voice said, "Quién es?"

Gould made his tone bruskly toneless—"Un mensajero. Tengo un paquete."

"Un momentito." There was the sound of a lock turning. The door opened a few inches, enough to frame the face of the singer Paquita. She extended a bare arm, said, "Démelo."

Then she recognized Gould.

For an instant shock held her motionless before she made an effort to slam the door shut. Gould already had his foot wedged inside. A thrust of his shoulder and he was inside the room.

Leaning back against the closed door he looked down at the girl. She had evidently been out of bed only a short time, not long enough to prepare herself for the day. Her face was still devoid of make-up; despite her obvious fear it had a warmer, more youthful look. She was wearing a black sleeveless nightdress of thin, nearly transparent material through which her figure was provocatively visible.

A moment passed in silence. She wet her lips, then swallowed with obvious effort.

"What is it you want?" Her voice was low, barely visible than a throaty whisper. "How did you get here?"

Gould smiled at her thinly without answering. Reaching behind him he snapped the door lock as he sent a searching glance around what was evidently the living room of the apartment. It was small, made more so by several heavy pieces of overstuffed Grand Rapids furniture. On the walls hung the usual religious chromos. It was a room without character, suggesting that the place had been rented furnished. There were two doors leading from the room. One was closed, the other open to reveal a small kitchen.

Paquita spoke again, her voice less muted by fear. "You have no right here. Get out. Get out before I——"

"Before you find out why I came?" Gould cut in. "That would be most foolish of you." He tore the loose wrapping from the lizard skin bag and held it out. "For one thing, I came to return your property."

Instinctively her hand reached out. Then she withdrew it quickly. "No. It's—it's not mine."

"Don't be stupid!" Gould tossed the handbag casually onto one of the easy chairs. "You're not exactly in a position to afford gestures like that. Now then, why? What was the big idea?"

"I don't know what you mean." Then, when Gould simply stared down at her with a thin smile, she burst out, "I don't understand any of it! It was all a horrible mistake!"

"That's better. Now suppose you go on explaining."

"No puedo." Belatedly she seemed to realize her near nakedness. She put a protective arm across her breasts.

"I can't tell you more. And you shouldn't be here talking to me like this. It isn't safe."

"For which one of us?"

"For you. For me. Por favor! Just take my word for it and go. But quickly!"

There was the sound of heavy footsteps in the hallway and Gould noticed the way in which she caught and held her breath until the steps passed. He said, "You are expecting someone?"

She nodded. "It will be very bad if you are found here. Bad for both of us."

"It is not your fault that I am here." Gould said reasonably. "Perhaps it is some one by the name of Ramón you are expecting?"

"Who told you that!"

Gould didn't answer. Instead he moved swiftly across the room, flung open the closed door, stood studying with searching eyes the small room beyond. There was an unmade double bed, a massive guardaropa with an inset oval mirror in one door, two straight-back chairs and a small table. On the floor by the side of the bed were crumpled stockings and a pair of high-heeled slippers. A light blue dress hung over the back of one of the chairs. The room was empty.

There was a key in the lock on the inside of the door. Gould extracted it. Then he turned to the girl who had remained motionless, watching him with wary eyes.

Gould made a short, imperative gesture with his thumb. "Inside."

She made no move to obey. Only the tone of her voice changed slightly. "What is it you intend?"

"Not what you apparently suspect," Gould told her. "This isn't exactly the time. You seem to fear having your friend Ramón find us together so I will meet him alone."

"No! You mustn't. You don't know Ramón when he is jealous angry. He will kill you! Go now—later I will tell you what little I know. I promise—"

She broke off suddenly. Footsteps again sounded in the hallway, pausing this time outside the apartment door. There was a light rap, then another. A voice called out, "Paquita."

The girl stood there, the fingers of one hand moving to her lips as though to guard their silence. Gould reached out, clamped a hand on one shoulder, spun her about and pushed her into the bedroom. He slammed the door shut and locked it, pocketing the key.

The knock was repeated, louder. The knob rattled. The voice said impatiently, "Paquita! Es Ramón. Abre!"

Gould put a hand under his jacket, loosened the Luger in its holster, moved over to one side of the door and snapped the lock open. He eased back so that the opening door concealed him.

Ramón Gómez stepped impatiently into the room. "Por qué tanta flojera, chula? No me digas que todavea estás durmiendo."

He swirled about at the sound of the door clicking shut and locking behind him. A number of expressions crossed his thin student's face—surprise, fear, suspicion. His right hand moved towards a hip pocket of his typical dark blue suit, hesitated, dropped to his side.

Gould waited.

Gómez's fiery brown eyes darted around the room. Finally he broke the tense silence. "What have you done with her?"

Gould jerked his head toward the bedroom door. "In there," Then, as Gómez started across the room he added tersely, "Locked in. No use trying the door. I have the key."

Gómez ignored him, rattling the door knob, calling out, "Paquita. Are you all right? Has the yanqui pig harmed you?"

For a moment there was no answer. Ramón Gómez half-turned his head, glaring at Gould over his shoulder, a look of sullen defiance crossed with worry. Then the sound of the girl's muffled voice came. "No. Leave me. Both of you. I want no trouble here."

Gómez turned fully, crying angrily. "You heard her. Leave. Now."

Slowly Gould shook his head. Without taking his eyes off Gómez he slipped a hand in a jacket pocket, pulled out a package of Casinos, shook one loose and put it between his lips. With the same slow deliberation he took out his Imco lighter, flicked it into flame. He inhaled deeply, expelling the smoke slowly through his nostrils.

"Why are you here?" Gómez demanded. "What is it you want?"

Bart Gould let another long moment go by. Then he said one word. "You."

"What for? There is nothing you can do to me. You are not of the police. Even if you were, I have nothing to fear."

"You can talk," Gould told him. "You love to talk. Now you. can talk to me. You can tell me what you know about the attempts on my life."

The air of nervous uncertainty left Gómez. Now, for the first time since entering the room, he seemed sure of himself.

"You are afraid, yanqui? Why don't you get out? Why don't you go back where you came from?" He spoke loudly, as though addressing an audience. For the girl's benefit, Gould decided. "We know what your plans are, yanqui. You want to keep this a tight little dictatorship, such as you have in Nicaragua and Honduras, where only you and your kind can profit. You want an excuse to interfere, as you did in Guatemala. I can promise you that this time you won't succeed, for all your careful plans."

"What plans?" Gould demanded coldly.

Gómez sneered at him. "You weren't as clever as you thought. We know what you are planning. It is even known where your people have their secret base. You have not been so clever, Señor Gould."

Gould's attention quickened, his mind flashing back to the fantastic story Titus Banning had told him in Washington of a planned demonstration of force using men with uniforms and weapons of the United States. He said carefully, "So you think you know——"

"It is known, have no doubt about that! Among your hirelings there are a few patriots who love their country more than they fear you."

As he listened to the man's pat, theatrically cliché phrases that sounded as though they had been taken out of some florid revolutionary handbook, Gould's thoughts raced ahead. That Gómez was only a minor figure in the conspiracy he was certain. Who was giving him orders? Who was pulling the puppets strings from behind the scenes? Most important of all, what actual information did he have?

He broke in harshly on Gómez's ranting. "Who ordered the attacks on me? Who persuaded you to endanger your girl friend in the attempts."

Ramón sent a nervous glance towards the locked bedroom door. "She was in no danger," he protested loudly.

"You say." Gould unbuttoned his jacket, allowed it to hang open. "Once again, who gave you your orders?"

Gómez's burning eyes flicked over the shoulder holster that had come into view. For a brief instant he seemed hesitant, wetting his lips with the tip of his tongue. Then with words he regained his courage. "Your gun does not frighten me. You cannot shoot me down in cold blood. You would not dare to. I am not afraid of death at your hands. I am of the people."

Gould's steel-grey eyes narrowed thoughtfully as he studied the man defying him. He recognized the type. Fanaticism crossed with a masochistic urge towards martyrdom. An almost psychopathic need to make grandiose gestures in the face of death. It was from men of this stamp that dedicated revolutionaries, the more unpleasant missionaires, and political crack-pots came.

Against such types ordinary threats had little effect.

Suddenly Gould's mind went back over the years to a time when he was in Kenya, visiting Ken Lawson, whose place was on the upper slopes of the Aberdares, in the middle of the Mau-Mau territory. The bloody uprising was at its height then, and he had been out with Ken one morning when a patrol from Fort Hall had brought in a captured Kikuyu terrorist. Gould had experienced a wave of shocked revulsion as he watched the systematic atrocities to which the Kikuyu was subjected in an effort to make him reveal the hiding place of his leader. "No point in threatening the blighter he'll be killed unless he talks," Lawson explained in a matter-of-fact tone as one of the man's eyes was gouged out. "He's bound by the *githaka* oath, which is a bloody obscene business. So normal reprisals don't mean a damned thing. You have to be as inhuman as these bastards themselves to get anywhere fighting them."

That's the way it is right now, Gould told himself. Against a fanatic such as Ramón Gómez ordinary threats wouldn't work. They never did.

Gómez was still talking loudly. "That is your country's answer to everything, isn't it, Señor Gould? A threat with a gun. But there are those who no longer bow down to such threats. I am one."

"You have a point," Bart Gould said with deceptive mildness. "It would be foolish to wave a gun in your face. As you say, you do not fear death." The lines on his hawk-like face suddenly tightened. His voice hardened. "But perhaps there is something else you fear."

Gómez eyed him suspiciously. "There is nothing—" He broke off sharply as he saw Gould's hand snake inside his jacket, come out holding a six-inch, double-edge knife.

"You recognize this?" Gould suggested. "It was used in the first attack on me yesterday. The one you involved your girl friend in. I intended returning it to you. Instead I am going to use it."

Staring at the gleaming knife blade, Gómez repeated mechanically, "I do not fear death."

"Who spoke of death? Not I." Gould's lips parted in a thin mockery of a smile. "I had something else in mind."

Slowly he began advancing across the room.

"No more empty words," he warned evenly. "You talk to me now, telling me that which I wish to know, or in the future when you speak all men will laugh at you. For shortly your voice will be that of a woman, for you will no longer be a man. You will sound and act like a maricon. Real men will mock at you and no woman will look at you twice."

"You joke. Such a thing is not possible—"

"I do not joke. And such a thing is very, very possible." Gould made a quick, indicative gesture with the knife blade. "So—and then so. Despues, un hombre sin conjones. A eunuch without virility. That will be you, my friend."

Gómez's lips moved, without sound. Brown-black eyes, wary and apprehensive, darted about the room seeking some way of escape. Finally he cried out, "You're mad. Loco—"

Then he lunged.

At the last split-second, Gould side-stepped. His left arm shot out like a steel piston, rock-hard fist hammer driving under Gómez's heart. As the man stumbled off-balance, Gould was on him, spinning him about, slamming him face-first against the wall. In the same movement, Gould slid the knife inside the man's trousers; a quick twist of the wrist and the razor-sharp blade sliced through waistband and belt.

Gould stepped back, spun Gómez about, drove in again with an elbow jammed against his throat and knee pressing upward in the groin.

"Talk!" he ordered. "Who directed the attacks against me?"

"I know nothing!" Gómez's fingers clutched at the empty air, seeking vainly to regain the pants that had fallen about his ankles. "I swear to God I know—"

He broke off with a thin gasp of fear as he felt the knife point prick the flesh of an inner thigh.

"Talk!" Gould commanded. "Talk while you can still speak in the voice of a man. The truth!" The knife point moved, probed, pressed.

"It was the German. Señor Norden."

"He gives you your orders?"

"I take orders from no man!" Then the knife point moved across the groin, cutting a thin path. Ramón cried out, "Yes. Yes. He gives suggestions. Advise. He is a man of vast experience. If harm comes to me you will pay for it!"

"That will not bring your manhood if you lose it." Gould's voice was harshly metallic. He let the knife point sink into flesh, drawing blood. Carefully he framed the next question. "Which hiding place for arms did you discover?"

"The only one."

"You think! There is more than one, you fool. Which one did you stumble across in your stupidity?"

For a moment it seemed to Gould as though Gómez were gathering his courage not to answer. Then words spilled out of him as though racing against the threat of the moving knife blade. "On your coffee finca. In the old bodega. The one at the ruined hacienda."

"You lie! There is nothing there."

"I saw it with my own eyes ..."

He'd had enough, Bart Gould decided. For long moments he had been half aware of fist hammering on the bedroom door and Paquita's voice sobbing out, "Stop! For the love of God stop whatever it is that you are doing!"

Gould withdrew his knife hand, stepped back. He allowed Gómez to slump forward, then caught him by the shirt front and sent him sprawling across the room.

Before he could regain his balance, Gould was on him again. A single short rabbit punch and he dropped unconscious to the floor.

For a brief moment Bart Gould stood staring down at him. Then he replaced the knife in his pocket, wiped his hands on his handkerchief, and quietly went out.

From now on, he decided ruefully, it wouldn't do to let Ramón Gómez get behind him on a dark night.

CHAPTER ELEVEN

IN THE taxi headed back to the hotel Bart Gould lit a Casino, inhaled deeply, let his mind dwell on the scene just finished. He was certain that even now Ramón Gómez was plotting revenge. But he was equally certain that by himself Gómez lacked effective means of exacting that revenge. He would depend on others, which meant that he would doubtlessly report back immediately to Norden, giving him a carefully edited account of what had taken place.

That was all right. Fine, in fact, if it meant that Norden would be forced to show his hand. Once again Gould reviewed the information he had forced out of Gómez, trying to fit it into place. If it were true that arms and uniforms were secreted somewhere on his finca, then that cleared up a good many things that had been puzzling him. It meant, for one thing, that his estate manager, Wagner, was in close alliance with Norden. It explained Wagner's uncharacteristic behavior—his unsummoned appearance at the hotel for the avowed purpose of saving Gould the trouble of making an immediate visit to his estates, followed by his curious insistence that Gould should sell out his holdings to some mysterious buyer.

Without doubt that unnamed buyer was Kurt Norden.

In all probability Norden was the mastermind behind the scheme to wreck the upcoming O.A.S. conference. That would mean it was Norden's agents who had noted and immediately reported his arrival in San Barrios, Norden's agents who had carried through the abortive attacks on him in an effort to get him out of the country. He remembered now the strangely flustered manner of the room clerk when he checked in at the Palace Hotel. Undoubtedly the man was part of Norden's network of agents and informers. And quite apparently his own unannounced appearance in San Barrios had posed a threat to carefully laid plans.

Now he could get a clearer picture of those plans. If a group of men, masquerading in the uniforms of American soldiers, was to be involved it would add credence to the business if it were later revealed that the group's secret base was on an estate owned by another American, Bartholomew Gould. It made sense. Moreover, it would be difficult to deny. Most Latin Americans, particularly those in the Central American countries, hadn't forgotten the not-too-secret training base sponsored by the C.I.A. in Guatemala prior to the ill-fated Bay of Pigs invasion.

If all that were so, it meant that there had been no leak in Washington as to the real purpose of his trip. It was simply coincidence that he had been indirectly drawn into the plot and that his presence now jeopardized its success. Then he wondered. It didn't do to underestimate Titus Banning's shrewdness, or the secret workings of his steel-trap mind. It was impossible that Banning had gambled that Gould, as a heavy property owner in San Barrios, would act as a lure to bring the plotters out into the open. No matter. The important thing now was that he was not only on the scene but apparently on the right track.

The taxi pulled to a stop in front of the Palace Hotel. Gould got out, paid off the driver, and stood for a moment of apparent indecision on the sidewalk, scanning the street as he lit a cigarette. Half a block down the avenue he spotted the dusty black shape of the Daimler. His eyes narrowed thoughtfully, then he shrugged, turned and went into the hotel.

There was one more errand he wanted to do before he drove out to his finca to see at first hand what was going on there. He stopped at the desk, picked up his key and announced loudly, "If any calls come in for me I'll be in the bar for a few minutes before I go up to my room."

He crossed the lobby, went through the swinging door into the cantina. It was just ten minutes short of twelve o'clock, at that early hour for drinking the place was nearly deserted. Gould walked up to the front end of the bar, close to the doors leading out onto the side street. The head barman who had been a fixture at the hotel ever since Gould could remember, left off a needless polishing of glasses and came over to greet him.

"Hace mucho tiempo que no venía por aquí, Don Bartolomé."

"A long time, Roberto," Gould agreed.

Roberto was already reaching for a bottle of ran negrita. "Lo de costumbre?"

"The same. You have a good memory, Roberto." Gould picked up the glass, drained half of it, then set it down on the bar. He snapped his fingers as though impatient with himself. "A better memory than I have. I've just remembered something. If anybody should want me I'll be back in half a minute."

He moved quickly out through the street doors. The Cord was parked a dozen yards from where De la Vega's man had left it earlier. Gould stood for a moment admiring its sleek power-packed body as he felt in his pocket for the keys. He had forgotten what a beauty the car was. This was the Model-810, one of the first hundred that had been hand-built for the New York auto show back in 1935. At that time some enthusiastic reporter had dubbed it 'sex on wheels' and the designation still held true, Gould decided. As he slid behind the wheel he scanned the aircraft-type instrument panel, fingered the electric pre-selector shift. With its front wheel drive it was the ideal car for sharply curving mountain roads.

He sat for a moment, mentally fixing the map of Colima and the outlying barrios in his mind, then started off. Magdalena, he recalled, was some fifteen kilometers away, just over the low range of mountains that bordered the city to the north. The road was thinly paved but otherwise unchanged from the curving, precipitous route first beaten out by pack burros centuries before.

Magdalena itself was no more than a huddle of 'dobe houses on narrow dirt roads leading off the highway. Gould turned in at the inevitable Taller Mecánico marked by two ancient gas pumps and asked directions of a man tinkering with the motor of an ancient Ford truck to the casa of Manuel Ortega.

The man indicated a small, newly white-washed house on the other side of the gas station. "There, señor. Pedro es demasiado tarde. Manuel murió hace ocho días."

"I know that. It is his widow I wish to speak with."

"Again you are too late, señor. She departed last evening."

"Where to?"

The man shrugged. "To some place on the other side of the country. It was all very sudden. A big car came for her and there was some story about a rich relative on the coast sending for her."

Gould's eyes narrowed thoughtfully. He took out cigarettes, offering one first to the mechanic. Then he flicked his lighter into flame, held it out. He said casually, "They say that Ortega was drinking heavily on the night of the accident."

"Mentiras! Manuel was here that very night, just an hour or so before it happened. He had driven out for cena with his wife and stopped here on his way back to check the air in his tires. He had had nothing to drink. Ni siquiera una cerveza!" The man puffed angrily on his cigarette. "I have heard such stories before but never have I encountered anyone who will say flatly that he saw Manuel drinking heavily that night or any other night."

Gould said, "You know Ortega's cousin, the one who has taken over his old job?" He frowned in concentration, trying to remember the man's name. "Enrique Anguilar, I think he is called."

The mechanic turned his head, spat into the dust with an expression of disgust. "That one! I have encountered him from time to time. But whatever else he may be, I can assure you that he is no relation to Manuel Ortega."

"So? Perhaps I misunderstood him. It would be interesting to know where he worked before."

"Everyone knows that, señor. He was always boasting of it. For the past two years or more he has been working for the German, the one who has the big land holdings across the lake."

Gould nodded as though the information was of no great significance.

Driving slowly back towards Colima, Gould decided that the trip out to Magdalena hadn't been entirely fruitless. He had wanted to talk to Ortega's widow and someone had gone to considerable effort to make sure she wasn't available. But there hadn't been any effective way to make sure that no one else in the barrio talked. It was a gamble that the other side was forced to take and had lost.

Every lead so far uncovered pointed to the German, Kurt Norden. But that solved nothing. There was no indication of what was actually at the base of the man's scheming. It seemed difficult to believe that Norden was operating on his own. What purpose would it serve his private interests to sabotage the O.A.S. conference and in so doing hold the United States up to world criticism as an inefficient meddler in Latin American affairs? The obvious next explanation was that

Norden was operating for some foreign power. Russia would be the obvious answer. The fact that Norden was reputed a man of wealth, a retired German capitalist, meant nothing. That could be only a front. But if Norden was in actuality a Soviet agent then he must be operating under an incredibly lax rein. It had been too easy to get on his trail and from all that Gould had ever heard about Soviet *agente provocateurs*—and he had heard a great deal over the years in Washington—they just didn't work that way.

Then he remembered stories he had heard in the Far East about Richard Sorge, the fantastic Soviet master-spy. By all accounts Sorge had violated every traditional rule for the successful espionage agent—he was a notorious lecher, a whore-master, a brawling, rambunctious drinker, creating one public scandal after another. Moreover, he had arrogantly and successfully defied the entire Communist bureaucracy, insisting on operating as a lone wolf reporting only to General Belden of the Fourth Bureau of the Red Army, the top-secret department concerned with espionage and plans for Soviet world domination. He had crowned his incredible career by becoming the trusted advisor to the German Ambassador Ott in Tokyo, helping to frame the Tri-Partate Agreement between Germany, Italy and Japan.

It just went to show that there were exceptions to every rule, and Burt Norden could well be one of those exceptions. You paid your money and you took your choice.

Gould parked the Cord behind the Palace Hotel, walked around to the side entrance to the bar. The drive out to Magdalena and back had taken a little over an hour. It was now a few minutes after one and the bar was well filled. Gould found a vacant space, elbowed his way in and waited until he caught Roberto's eye.

The barman poured out a glass of dark rum, brought it over and placed it in front of Gould. In a low voice he said, "There have been several inquiries from the hotel desk. I said that you would be back in a moment."

Gould nodded, downed his drink and left a ten peso note on the bar.

The lobby was more crowded now. There was a cluster of people around the reception desk with a small mountain of luggage at one side. As he crossed the lobby Gould caught snatches of the liquid cadences of Brazilian-Portuguese. More delegates for the O.A.S. conference, he decided, and wondered what the latest Brazilian rumors about the future plans of Janio Quadros might be. He ignored the elevator, taking the wide curving stairs up to the second floor.

When he opened the door to his suite and stepped inside he discovered a visitor waiting.

CHAPTER TWELVE

CLARE HAMMET was sitting in the room's one comfortable easy chair. The ash tray on the table at one side was heaped high with half-smoked, filter tip cigarettes.

Evidently she had been waiting a long time.

Gould leaned back against the door, silently looking across the room with a politely raised eyebrow.

Clare Hammet said quickly, "I hope you don't mind my taking the liberty of waiting for you up here. The lobby is a little too public and might cause gossip."

"Naturally," Gould agreed while the thought drifted through his mind that the discovery of an ambassador's wife surreptitiously visiting a hotel room might cause even more gossip. "One can't be too careful."

She gave him a quick, searching glance as though trying to detect a hint of mockery in his even tones. "It was important that I see you as soon as possible."

"I'm honored," Gould told her. "Even though slightly mystified." He walked across the room, turned one of the cumbersome straight-backed chairs around so it faced her. He said, "I regret that I can not be much of a host. Under the circumstances I take it that you wouldn't care for me to call down to room service for something pleasant in the way of refreshments. All I have here is black rum and most women find it much too heavy."

She started to make an automatic gesture of refusing and then suddenly appeared to change her mind. "I am not most women,

Mr. Gould. I think I should like to try some of this famous rum of yours."

Gould went into the bedroom for the bottle he had left on the dresser and then on into the bathroom for glasses. Now what? he asked himself. Just what is in the wind? He shrugged mentally, deciding the answer would come soon enough.

Back in the living room he poured out two half glasses of ron negrita. As he handed her a glass he said, "There's a carafe of agua filtrada if you'd like a chaser."

She shook her head, smiling at him over the rim of her glass. "I like most things straight, Mr. Gould."

I'll let that one ride, Gould told himself. He raised his glass. "Zum wohle."

Automatically she started to answer in kind. "Zum—" She broke off suddenly, frowned, asked with a little laugh of protest, "But why do you address me in German? I know next to nothing of the language."

Gould smiled. "My subconscious at work, I suppose. Possibly because you have a type of classic Nordic beauty."

"I thank you." She hesitated, her eyes watching him. "My grandmother was Scandinavian and I am supposed to take after her." She waited, and when Gould simply continued smiling politely at her, went on, "You are wondering why I am here. It is because I am wondering the same thing about you."

"I thought I explained that yesterday at luncheon. Simply because I haven't been down here for several years and I don't approve of being an absentee landlord. What other reason could I possibly have?"

Clare Hammet's clear blue eyes studied him intently. Again she shook her head slightly. "Your appearance is too—shall we say, fortuitous, Mr. Gould. You came down here directly from

Washington. You must have learned there that the political situation in San Barrios is extremely tense."

"As I said before, my only connection with Washington is that I happen to own a home there."

Her lips curved in a faint smile of disbelief. "And that is why you were so interested in details of poor Hobart Drake's accidental death? That is why you wanted to visit the driver's home to ask questions of his widow? Even without a woman's intuition, Mr. Gould, I would suspect otherwise."

Instead of answering, Gould slowly finished the remainder of his drink. What was all this leading up to, he asked himself. What the hell was the purpose of this visit?

He kept an expression of polite interest on his face as he poured another drink.

Clare Hammet went on slowly, "If it is true that you are only here by pure happenstance, then you could do me a very great favor, Mr. Gould." She paused, before adding softly, "You would find me most appreciative."

She leaned forward slightly, partly turning with a sensuous slowness to face him more fully, letting her body emphasize the unspoken significance of her words.

Even as he became warily alert, Gould found himself judging her performance with critical objectivity. His eyes flickered over the now slightly exposed breasts revealed as she bent over, the sleekly voluptuous outline of her long legs only faintly masked by the clinging material of her light jersey dress. Once again he was aware of the subtle fragrance of Patou's Joy and considered vaguely how the wife of a minor ambassador could afford such extravagances. At the same time he asked himself why it was that most women thought that they could immediately become sexually appealing simply by calling attention to their bodies.

"And the favor?" he asked, realizing as he did so that she had adroitly prepared a neat little trap for him.

"Leave here at once." She made a quick gesture with one hand as though to stop him from interrupting her. "If you are here simply because you have nothing better to do, then leave and come back at some other time."

"Why should I do that?"

She gave him another long, searching look. "I still cannot believe that you are as ignorant of what is taking place here as you pretend. If you are, then I should not discuss information of which only the Embassy is aware. But I can tell you this. The situation here is explosive. My husband's career and reputation are both at stake. When this O.A.S. conference is over things may go back to normal but until then—" She spread out her hands in a gesture of appeal. "It is difficult to explain but believe me, it would be better if you left the country."

Gould regarded her with an expression of blank puzzlement. "You mystify me. I don't see how my presence here even at this particular time can upset anyone. It never has before."

"Can't you just take my word for it? If not, consider this. You own considerable properties here and that means that you are an emblem of the foreign capitalist from the North against which there is so much feeling now. This is no time to flaunt such a hated emblem in front of the masses."

Gould permitted himself a half-smile. "I hadn't realized that I had automatically become so unpopular."

"Hadn't you noticed any signs of it?"

Gould masked any tell-tale expression that might be crossing his face as he busied himself lighting a cigarette. He wondered if she were referring obliquely to the two attempts so far made on his life. He shrugged slightly. "I really hadn't noticed anything."

He was watching her intently and was certain he detected a look of surprise, followed quickly by one of suspicious doubt, flash across her face. He added half-apologetically, "Of course, I don't go looking for such things so it may be that I overlooked any evidence of unfriendly feeling."

"I can't believe you are quite that obtuse, Mr. Gould." Her voice held a note of impatience which she immediately seemed to regret. She picked up her glass, sipped again at the rum, and went on in a more seductive tone, "It is really very little that I ask. And I told you that you would find me most appreciative."

If it is so little that you ask how is it that you are offering so much in return, Gould was prompted to reply.

She stood up slowly, her movements languid and lazily sensual, and walked over to where he was standing. She stood close to him, looking up at him with eyes that were suddenly soft with promise. She said in a voice that was almost a muted whisper, "I've heard about you, Bart Gould. I've heard about you—and some of the women you have known. I wonder if it is all true ..."

Her voice trailed off. She took the glass out of Gould's hand and placed it on the table. She moved closer until her body was against his and she could put her arms about his neck.

Gould felt her body molding itself artfully against his—felt the pressure of her breasts and the slow, almost imperceptible movement of her hips as they pressed forward.

He let his hands move down her body, let her lips burn hotly for the space of a long kiss.

Then he thrust her firmly away.

He said lightly, "One thing your friends forgot to tell you about me, my dear Clare."

She stared back at him through sultry, doubtful eyes. "Yes?"

"I dislike matinées. I was brought up to believe they were only for suburbanites who had to catch a train and I dislike being hurried." He moved away, picked up his glass, and added, "Almost as much as I dislike attempts to bribe me."

As she headed for the door, Clare Hammet said angrily, "You'll regret this!"

"I'm sure," Gould said politely.

CHAPTER THIRTEEN

HE ATE a brief and uninspired luncheon in the overcrowded dining room of the hotel. Then he went out through the bar again.

He had just started the motor of the Cord when he heard someone calling out his name.

It was the singer Paquita, half-running down the sidewalk in his direction.

"Señor Gould. Por favor—un momentito."

Just what was the set-up this time, Gould wondered. The girl reached the car just as he shifted into gear. She rested her hands on the door, paused for a moment to catch her breath, "Wait, please. It is a matter of importance."

"I'm sure," Gould said. "But not tonight, Josephine."

He put out a hand and firmly flicked her fingers from the car door. As he let out the clutch and turned into the traffic he heard her cry after him, "You don't understand! I came to warn you …"

Then blaring horns drowned out her words and Gould dismissed her from his mind.

Under normal conditions it was a good five hour drive from Colima to the southwestern border of Lago Cristobal. The trouble was that conditions were seldom normal on many stretches of the road. Like most Central American countries, San Barrios had only a few paved highways and the road sweeping around the mountains bordering the lake was not one of these roads. The greater portion of its 240 kilometer length was narrow, rocky, ungraded. In the valleys portions were unpassable during the rainy season, there were stretches over the mountains so narrow that two vehicles could not pass.

But in the Cord that clung tenaciously to the dirt slippery, treacherous mountain curves, Gould figured that with luck he could shave the driving time by close to an hour.

Even so, it would be after nightfall when he reached his destination.

Gould was aware of an inner tenseness. His fingers wrapped too tightly around the wheel. He forced himself to relax. This type of edginess, this impatience for definite action, did no good. It was poor tactics to dwell at too much length on the unknown. Far better to consider the facts at hand and their significance.

He thought again about Clare Hammet and her surreptitious visit to his hotel room. How deeply was she involved in the business? With some women, particularly ambitious women, it was hard to tell what was really at the root of their actions. They could always rationalize the most incredible behaviour with feminine logic. He wished he had some immediate way of discovering more of her background. He had a feeling that a part of it, perhaps the most important part of it, was carefully cloaked in vague generalities. He wondered where and how Roger Hammet had first met her.

He wondered again what the real purpose behind her visit had been. Was it to discover exactly how much he knew? Was she, too, tied up in some way with the mysterious German, Kurt Norden? And did Roger Hammet, himself, have any inkling of his wife's activities?

Well, one thing was definite, he told himself as he negotiated a sharp turn. Up until that morning there could only have been uncertain suspicion as to the exact reason for his being in San Barrios. But following his session with Ramón Gómez there could now be Little doubt. By now Gómez had unquestionably reported back to his superiors his own highly colored, carefully edited account of that morning.

The final cards in this strange poker game had been dealt. From now on it was a game without limit.

The brief twilight of a tropic night came as he negotiated the final hairpin turns of a mountain descent and leveled out on a long stretch of road that bordered the lake.

It was now just a matter of forty kilometers to the turn-off leading to his hacienda. A matter of twenty minutes at the most, always providing he encountered no other vehicle on the road.

Just once was he forced to slow down to a crawl to edge through a small herd of goats. Then he was turning in to the mile long driveway leading to the old buildings of the hacienda. He let the Cord ease to a stop in the outer courtyard. He flicked off the headlights and sat motionless for a moment behind the wheel. Something was wrong, he felt intuitively. Where normally there should be workers and servants moving about there was now no sigh of activity. Instead a feeling of hidden movement held in hushed suspense.

He got out of the car and walked across the stone-flagged courtyard. A hazy spread of light from the ancient Spanish carriage lamps set in the thick wall on either side of the massive doorway of carved teak fought a losing battle with the surrounding night shadows.

He raised a hand to the heavy wrought iron knocker, then noticed that the double doors were slightly ajar.

He pushed one open, stepped into the wide entrance foyer. The wall lights were on, shedding a soft glow over the pieces of early Spanish armor that had that been a fixture in the hallway for as far back as Gould could remember.

He called out for the house servants that had once seemed to have been there almost as long. “María! Ramona! Domingo!”

There was no answer.

Gould hesitated, a frown creasing his forehead. Then he strode across the wide hallway, opened the door leading into the main sala of the building. Here, too, the lights were on. He saw his estate manager, Guillermo Wagner, standing at one side of the room, his hands resting on the back of a chair.

Gould stopped short and glared at him. “What the hell goes on here! Where are the servants?”

Wagner didn’t answer. His eyes slid away from Gould and across the room. Gould half turned his head.

There was a stranger sitting in the far corner of the room behind the mahogany refectory table that Gould and his uncle before him had always used as a working desk. A small man with skin the color of pale parchment. His eyes were concealed behind dark glasses. A Basque beret was fitted tightly on his head.

The man finished fitting a cigarette into a slim ivory holder before he spoke in studiously accented English. “Good evening, Mr. Gould. We have been awaiting your arrival.”

“So I see.” Gould made no attempt to keep a tone of sarcasm from his voice. “I trust the courtesies of the house have been properly extended.”

“Most satisfactorily, thank you.” The man’s glance flicked toward the silent Wagner. “But I fear your manager is neglecting his duties. He has failed to perform the appropriate introductions.”

“My former manager,” Gould corrected sharply. “I think we can do without his services, can we not, Herr Norden?” He turned his attention back to Wagner. “You heard me. You’re through. Now get the hell out of here.”

Wagner looked at him and then away without moving. Norden said, "I am afraid you no longer are in a position to give orders here, Mr. Gould."

The lines on Bart Gould's face tightened. "And just what gives you that idea?"

The German made a negligent gesture with the cigarette holder. An ash fell on the polished surface of the table and he brushed it neatly off. "Because this is no longer your property." He raised a hand as though to cut short an expected interruption. When none came he went on evenly, "True, the transfer of the property deeds is not a matter of public record as yet but that is a formality that can be taken care of without difficulty."

"There is also the little matter of my signature to any property transfer," Gould said coldly. "That may not be so easily acquired."

"You are mistaken. There are ways of obtaining it which I would prefer not to go into now. All this is trouble of your own making, Mr. Gould. You could have avoided it so very easily."

"I tried to prevent it," Wagner spoke up for the first time. "I made the trip into Colima in order to give you a chance to sell out without getting yourself involved. You wouldn't listen to me."

Gould said, "Are you going to get out of here or do I have to throw you out!"

He took a step towards his estate manager. Norden's voice warned sharply, "No violence, please. It is not yet the time for it. If you doubt me glance over your shoulder, Mr. Gould."

Gould turned his head. Two men had entered the room behind him and stood silently waiting. One was of medium height, with the flat, emotionless features of a Mayan. He was carrying a Garand rifle as though it were as much a part of his accustomed equipment as a machete had been to his ancestors. It was pointed directly at Gould.

The other man was the dwarf who had caught Gould's attention getting into the big Daimler the day before. Then he had been wearing a straw sombrero and Gould had only noticed his grotesquely misshapen body. Now he was hatless and Gould saw with a shock of disgust the obscene ugliness of the man—the shaven skull ridged with layers of yellow fat, the sunken pig eyes, the flattened nose that was only indicated by the black pits of his nostrils. Criss-crossed cartridge belts draped his thick waist, supporting holsters that hung two-thirds of the way down his bowed dwarf legs. The holsters were now empty, the .45 automatics in the dwarf's hands.

Gould studied the two figures for a silent moment before he turned back to Norden. "Part of your family, I presume? No introductions are needed."

The pale parchment face of the German darkened momentarily. Then he regained control of himself. "It pleases you to try my patience, Mr. Gould. I would advise against so indulging yourself."

Gould stood there in the center of the familiar room that had now taken on a curious menacing strangeness, staring through narrowed eyes at this stranger who seemed so sure of himself. He said flatly, picking his words with care, "Suppose we stop talking in circles and get to the point. Exactly what do you want?"

"You pretend not to know?"

"Frankly I don't."

Norden shook his head. "It is too late to take that stand. Twenty-four hours ago I might have believed that it was simply an unfortunate coincidence that you happened to choose this particular time to visit San Barrios. But you managed quite effectively to remove any doubts I might have entertained, Mr. Gould. Your actions since your arrival have given you away."

"What actions?"

"Need I enumerate? In some ways you have been too clever, and in other ways not clever enough. You have been quick to get on the trail of certain of my associates but at the same time you have asked too many questions of the wrong people. You have become an obstacle to my plans. But an obstacle that can both be removed and made use of."

As he listened, apparently oblivious to the implied threat, Gould's mind worked with feverish speed. His left arm pressed against the slim bulk of the shoulder holster. He tried to estimate to a fine degree what his chances would be if he went for the Luger, swirled and shot it out with the two men standing behind him. The odds were not too good, he decided. While his back was turned he would be a perfect target for either Norden or Wagner, and the possibility was strong that both were armed. Moreover, the stakes were too high—it wasn't his life alone that might be forfeited but the vital interests of his country. For the moment the only sensible thing to do was to stall for time.

He shrugged. "All this is very dramatic, but it still doesn't make sense. Naturally I'm concerned with looking after my own interests and it was apparent that someone was interfering with them. It didn't take too long to discover that you were the one. I still want to know why."

The German studied him appraisingly, as though debating some problem with himself. Finally he made one of his abrupt gestures with his cigarette holder. "Why not? Whatever you know, or suspect that you know, can only be a small portion of the truth. It would give me a certain pleasure to inform you more fully of what I have in mind over dinner. I will tell you everything, Mr. Gould, for it sometimes is helpful to explain things one has kept too long to oneself." He paused, then added almost as an afterthought, "And the information can do you no good, nor me any harm. For you will not live long enough to make use of it."

CHAPTER FOURTEEN

AN HOUR later Bart Gould was still seated at his own dinner table, now presided over by Kurt Norden. Several things had happened before then. He had been quickly and efficiently searched, relieved of the Luger and the knife he was still carrying in his breast pocket. He had made a point of refusing to sit down at the table if Wagner was to be present at dinner.

"I refuse to sit at the same table with that schweinehund," he had stormed. "I have never associated socially with half-breeds and do not intend to start now."

In part it was an act, in part he was trying to see how accurately he had judged the character of the man Norden. By now he was certain that he had placed his accent. It was the harsh German of the Junkers of the North Prussia of landed estates from which the hard core of the German High Command of the old days had sprung. Such men were sticklers for a caste system—always providing, of course, that they were at the top.

As a result only Norden and Gould were at the table. The flat-faced, silent Indian stood in the shadows of one corner, holding the rifle in a crook of his arm. Norden half apologized for his presence. "A necessary precaution, Mr. Gould. Although you are unarmed I do not quite trust you."

"Perhaps you are wise," Gould said evenly.

The German had finally removed the beret and dark glasses, revealing pale, whitely blue eyes and a high student's forehead across which ran an ugly, livid scar that drew the skin towards it in uneven puckers.

The meal had been served by servants unfamiliar to Gould, and had been plain but adequate. Only the wines had been exceptional and those Gould strongly suspected had come from his own private stock.

Now Norden repeated his previous remark that had brought a grunt of ridicule from Gould.

"I repeat, I intend to become the absolute ruler of all of Latin America."

"That's a full-sized ambition."

"You think it an extravagant one? It is so only in scope. Anything is possible if an intelligent man puts his mind to it. Look what a penniless journalist named Mussolini managed to achieve. Look what an Austrian derelict by the name of Hitler who received his education in the slums of Vienna managed to do."

"Look at them now," Gould suggested drily.

Norden dismissed their fate with a flick of his fingertips. "They were victims of their own ambitions and lack of background. They had no solid plan."

"And you have?"

Norden nodded. "You listen, but you do not believe. I assure you, it is most simple. This little demonstration I have worked out—this sabotage of the O.A.S. conference and the implication of your government—a demonstration, I might say, that you are powerless now to hinder—is but a minor move in an over-all plan. Simply a way of demonstrating my power for the benefit of those whose aid I expect to enlist."

"All for the benefit of a new and better Nazi Germany, I suppose?" Gould remarked.

Norden's lips twisted into a thin, bitter smile. "Unfortunately, that would be a waste of time. Europe, the old Europe, is kaput. Finished. A dry bone for your government and Russia to snarl over. Latin America, on the other hand, has everything that Europe now lacks. Natural resources in abundance. Room for expansion. It is not decadent and worn out, as is Europe. Moreover the time is now ripe for the type of central power I have in mind." He paused and took a sip of wine. He held the glass under his nose for an appreciative moment. "I must compliment you on your cellar here, Mr. Gould. This is an excellent Liebfraumilch, one of our better Rhine wines."

Gould made an appropriate reply. Behind the facade of his politely sceptical interest, his mind was worrying the problem facing him. That Norden was both a fanatic and in deadly earnest there was little doubt. Now, his pale blue eyes feverishly alight, he was saying, "All of Latin America finally united under one dynamic ruler! A major power in the world. The final major power, once your country and Russia have engaged in the inevitable suicidal war. That is something to think about, is it not?"

Deliberately Gould goaded him with a mocking laugh. "It is an amusing day-dream."

"It is more than that. It is on the threshold of being a reality. Your country thinks of Latin America as being within its sphere of influence while it does everything to destroy whatever influence it might have. You pour out gold but not your trust. Even while you talk of friendship you allow your politicians and some of your most powerful publications to deride and belittle the Latin American countries. You make it very easy to build up an anti-American feeling."

"It will take something more positive to achieve what you have in mind."

"Naturally. But I said before that the time is now ripe. The governments are shaky in Argentine and Brazil, in Ecuador and Columbia. And elsewhere. The civilian rulers have failed. The military is once again moving in or about to move in. And with the military cliques one can always do business. It is a matter of understanding their mentality. They will support any government just so long as it does not encroach on their power and privilege. So one caters to them until they are no longer needed."

"That sounds like a lesson you learned well from Hitler."

For the second time that evening the pale parchment of Norden's face darkened with a wave of repressed anger. A full moment passed before he said coldly, "There were reasons for the attitude of the High Command in those days. Matters of tradition that you would not be expected to understand."

"It seems to me that I have heard that before." Gould studied the bowl of fruit that had been placed on the table, selected a pear and began to peal it. Again he played with an idea that had intrigued him all through the meal. He wondered if with one lightening move he could flip the fruit knife across the table so that it would find a vital spot in the German's throat. But that would still leave the impassive Indian standing in the corner, cradling the Garand rifle. It wasn't worth the chance. Moreover, there was still information that Gould wanted. He said slowly, "There is still something I don't quite believe. Your man G6mez accused me of secreting American arms and uniforms here on the hacienda. I can believe readily enough that there are arms here but that they can be identified as coming from the United States I find hard to swallow."

Norden gave a pleased laugh. "Gómez is not one of my trusted men. Merely a pawn, useful for creating diversions to distract official eyes. He hasn't any faint idea of what it is all about. But in that one respect he was accurate in what he told you."

Gould managed to look doubtful.

Norden was boasting now. "The arms of any particular country are the easiest things in the world to obtain. The big nations are constantly selling off surplus weapons. There are men in Zurich and Brussels who can furnish you anything from small arms to heavy tanks and jet planes, and in any quantity. One of your own compatriots, with his headquarters in Monaco and offices in Geneva and Zurich, can supply anything to anyone. And it is all legitimate or very nearly so. In the matter of army uniforms it is even simpler. Your own government regularly offers a surplus for sale at bargain prices. If you could take a look inside of the old mill, on the border of your estate, you would find it most adequately stocked for a minor skirmish."

He broke off, took a delicate sip of brandy, added arrogantly, "It is only a matter of taking intelligent advantage of the stupidity of others. There will be certain other demonstrations of my power to control and destroy that need not be disclosed at present, although your government is aware of them."

Gould remembered suddenly Titus Banning's disclosure that, along with everything else, a threat had been made to bomb the Panama Canal. Now that threat seemed far less fantastic than it had sounded in Banning's austere office in the White House. He kept his expression and his tone coldly sceptical. "I'll take your word for it."

"You would be wise to. I regret only that you will not be with us to appreciate it."

Gould shrugged. His hands were resting on the edge of the table. His fingers tightened slightly as he remembered that the table was of solid teak, some inch and a half thick. Not bulletproof, exactly, but it was wood sufficiently hard to blunt the impact of any slugs.

It was worth a gamble, he decided swiftly. On the moment of rising one sudden, decisive movement could upend the table, giving him temporary shelter while he made a dive for Norden's legs. With the German in his grasp, the Indian wouldn't dare fire.

He waited, nerves tense, for the precise moment. Finally it came. Norden put down his empty brandy glass, dabbed his thin white lips with a napkin, signaling that the dinner was at an end.

Gould tightened his grasp on the table's edge. He started to rise. At the last minute he saw the German's eyes flicker over his shoulder, heard a faint sound behind him.

He ducked instinctively, trying to turn at the same place.

He was too late.

There was a split second of agonizing pain as something struck the back of his head with terrific force. He felt himself falling forward.

Then he lost consciousness.

CHAPTER FIFTEEN

CONSCIOUSNESS RETURNED slowly. The wave of blackness that had engulfed him was replaced by a heavy murky grey.

Bart Gould became increasingly aware of the ache of cramped muscles and a dull pain at the back of his head. He opened his eyes slowly, instinctively remaining motionless, trying to probe the heavy gloom. At first there was nothing recognizable. Only a vastness of shadowy space, apparently without beginning or end.

He put his hands down, felt the gritty hardness of baked earth beneath him. Carefully he reached to one side. His searching fingers encountered nothing.

He tried with the other hand. This time he touched the rough surface of crudely hewn stone. Once again with narrowed eyes he studied the anonymous grey darkness. There was no sign of a window, of an opening of any kind.

He forced himself to concentrate, to picture in his mind the layout of the sprawling hacienda buildings and rooms. As nearly as he could judge he must be in one of the old unused bodegas.

He tried to remember what had happened. The last thing he could recall was rising from the dinner table with some plan of a sudden surprise attack against the German well fixed in his mind.

Then had come quick oblivion. Somebody had crept silently behind him and struck him down before he could put that plan into effect.

He moved restlessly now, tapping his pockets. He still had cigarettes and his lighter. He stuck a cigarette in his mouth and flicked the lighter. By its flame he saw that his suspicion had been correct, he was in one of the old bodegas. The one located on one side of the outer work patio, if his memory was correct. He remembered, too, that the stone walls were a foot thick and the heavy doors strongly reinforced with iron bars.

The place was as solid as an old-time fortress. And as escape-proof.

He was halfway through his cigarette when he heard a sound outside. There was a protesting creak of iron hinges as one side of the bodega doors swung open. Gould started to move, but not quickly enough. The beam of a strong electric torch pinned him down in a circle of eye-smarting white light.

He closed his eyes for a quick moment, then opened them behind a shielding hand.

He heard the voice of the German. "You may put the torch on the floor, Pepe. Our guest seems not to care for the spotlight."

Gould took another puff on his cigarette and said nothing. With the light deflected slightly he could see the squat figure of the dwarf standing to one side of Norden. The latter was once again wearing the tight beret and the dark glasses. Habit, Gould wondered, or vanity?

Now Norden addressed him directly. "I trust you have fully recovered from your little—" He hesitated. "Shall we say accident of last night? I looked in earlier and you were still unconscious. I fear that sometimes Pepe is a bit too enthusiastic about carrying out routine orders."

Gould remained silent.

"It was needed precaution, you know," Norden went on smoothly. "I had a feeling that you were contemplating some stupid move. I did not wish to have you shot down by the Indian, Mario. It would have upset certain of my plans."

Gould allowed himself a faint grunt. "That's nice to know."

"You do not seem appreciative of moments added to your life. I assure you that if necessary I can change the plans I have for you."

"For God's sake stop talking like an imitation Himmler!" Gould snapped his cigarette butt away. "Get to the point. What plans?"

"I think your nerves are on edge, my friend. But then, lack of self-control is a typical American failing. I have several things in mind. For one, I think it would be most appropriate if you should be killed leading the group of American soldiers who are scheduled to spearhead an attempted uprising against the present government. It is a matter that can be most easily arranged."

"I have no doubt."

"But there are other affairs to be attended to first. The matter of your signature on certain papers, for example. True enough, the signature can be forged but I much prefer to have everything strictly legal in the event of too close an investigation by the authorities of your country later on."

"You can be certain of the investigation," Gould promised grimly.

"There are ways and means of persuasion." Norden licked his thin lips, his voice taking on the tone of a gourmet remembering the menu of a Cordon Bleu dinner. "The old days of the rack and the thumb screw are not as out-of-date as some people would like to think. Unfortunately we lack such equipment here. But there are other means, always close at hand. Castor oil, for example, so readily available here. Administered by the liter the effects are remarkable. Internal haemorrhages and ruptures that never show on the surface but that can cause a most unpleasant death.

Then there is the rubber hose, which I understand is a favorite of your police departments. That, too, leaves no incriminating outward marks. I wouldn't want there to be any suspicion as to the actual cause of your death, señor Gould, if you should prove too unreasonably stubborn."

"Thoughtful of you," Gould said.

"I believe so." Norden became suddenly sharply precise. "I will leave you now to think matters over. I must return to my own place. I shall be back either tonight or early in the morning. I trust that by then you have decided to act wisely. There is no point in needless suffering." He started to turn away, then checked himself to add in a mockery of manners, "Allow me to thank you again for your hospitality."

"The visit will be returned in kind," Gould assured him.

"I wouldn't count on it. The dwarf, Pepe, will serve you your meals and guard you during my absence. I sincerely advise you not to attempt anything stupid. He is a man—or let us say a creature—who quite literally does not know his own strength. And it would be equally useless to try to bribe him. He is completely faithful to me."

"In that case you are correct in suggesting that he is subhuman," Gould said. "Even so, I am beginning to have the feeling that his company might prove preferable."

The German stood silently for a moment, then turned on his heel and marched out, followed quickly by the dwarf.

The heavy door slammed shut.

Once again Gould was left in semi-darkness with only his thoughts for company.

He lit another cigarette and sat quietly smoking while he considered his next move. Finally he got up and sparingly flicking his lighter on and off made a thorough tour of the bodega.

He encountered nothing that could be used as a weapon.

Checking the time he saw that it was nine-thirty and remembered that he had had no breakfast. At the same time he remembered something else. Norden had warned him that the dwarf, Pepe, was a creature who didn't know his own strength. It had been meant as a threat but it revealed something more, that Pepe must be under orders not to kill him out of hand.

Gould sat down and waited.

It was ten minutes later when he heard the bodega doors opening. Once again an electric torch momentarily blinded him until it was placed on the floor. Pepe advanced a few steps, put a basket down on the floor, grunted, "Su desayuno."

"Bring it here, pig!" Gould snapped. "Perhaps I should teach you how scum like you should behave."

He got up, took a staggering step forward, deliberately slipped and fell, landing on his back.

The dwarf laughed—an animal, gutteral sound like a throaty gargle. He came closer, aiming a scornful kick at Gould's ribs.

Gould had drawn up his knees in a protective gesture. Now he turned slightly, waited for the precise moment, then shot both heels with pile-driver force upwards into the dwarf's crotch.

Lifted into the air, the dwarf sailed backward, Gould was up and on him almost before he landed, driving a knee down into the muscle-hard belly. There was a grunt of painfully expelled breath.

The .45 the dwarf had been holding slithered onto the ground. Gould longed to reach for it, send a bullet through the head of the obscene monster twitching beneath him, but he dared not risk the sound of a shot. Instead he wrapped his fingers around the bull neck, thumbs pressing relentlessly down on the wind pipe.

Beads of sweat stood out on his forehead as he forced added strength into his fingers, felt them sink into slowly yielding flesh.

The squat, malformed body beneath him gave a final convulsive shudder and then was still.

Gould stood up slowly, wiping the sweat from his forehead with the back of a hand. He bent down, picked up the .45 from the ground, then unloosened the cartridge belts and holsters from the dwarf's middle and put them on.

Now he had two guns. The odds against whatever awaited him outside were a little more even.

He walked over to the heavy, iron-reinforced double doors, lifted the locking bar, eased one of the doors gently open. The sudden glare of white-hot sunlight reflected on the white walls surrounding the outer patio made his eyes blink in protest. Glancing down at the Rolex on his wrist he saw that it was just a few minutes past ten.

He stood in the shelter of the open doorway for a long moment, considering his next move. He thought of going back into the main house, then ruled against it. There was the possibility that Norden and some of his henchmen might still be there and there were more important matters to be attended to before he tangled with the German again.

He swung the heavy door shut, slipped the massive padlock back into place and snapped it shut. With luck there would be a delay now before his escape was discovered—time that he needed badly.

Keeping close to the bodega he began moving towards a side wall where an iron gate opened out into a small field of alfalfa. He had just reached it when he heard a warning shout.

Gould spun about. Wagner was standing on the far side of the patio, reaching for the gun dangling at his hip.

Gould reacted instinctively. Without conscious thought a .45 was in his hand and being fired.

The first shot caught Wagner in the throat as he opened his mouth to shout again. With cold eyes Gould watched his head jerk back, saw the body topple backwards in slow motion to the ground.

He opened the gate, then stood for a space of seconds listening intently for any sounds from the main house. He heard only the barking of one of the dogs.

Slowly, still keeping close to the protecting outer wall enclosing the hacienda buildings, Gould began moving toward the thick tangled undergrowth of what had once been a forest of mahogany. There was a winding, little used dirt road that led around to the old mill, but Gould recalled that it was some twenty kilometers in length. But from his earlier years, Gould recalled that there was a short cut through the forest that more than halved the distance.

He wondered if he could remember it; wondered, too, if it had long since been obliterated by the fecund growth of the tropics.

There was only one way of finding out.

Not until he reached the edge of the forest and was safely deep in the concealing underbrush did he draw an easy breath. At any moment he had expected to hear the sharp crack of a rifle, his very spine had itched in protest against being so inviting a target.

Now he hesitated, thinking back, trying to get his bearings. Finally he forced his mind into a blank, started moving automatically, letting his sub-conscious memory take over. After ten minutes of tortuous pushing through a matted tangle of undergrowth he began to curse the dead Wagner for letting the forest revert to a jungle.

Then his feet found the old trail, recognizable only because the growth was thinner. Clearly it had been used in recent times but not often enough to keep down the encroaching mass of creeper vines and thick shrubs. Thorny branches tore at Gould's clothing, whipped in flesh-tearing scratches across his face and arms. Swarms of gnats and mosquitoes kept him unwelcome company as he pushed relentlessly on. He recalled once, on his first trip to Africa, moving with the same grim determination through the trackless jungles along the Uaso Nyrio River.

This was a different kind of safari, with a different kill as the final goal.

CHAPTER SIXTEEN

ONCE, BEFORE the revolutions that swept the country at the turn of the century, the old mill had been used to grind the corn and wheat that the Indians brought in from the outlying milpas. Its location, distant as it was from the main hacienda, had been a matter of expediency, the ancient water wheel turned by a narrow stream that raced down toward the lake from a mountain spring. During the last half a dozen decades it had been allowed to fall into ruins.

It was a full two hours later before a slight rise in the ground told Gould he was approaching the site. He slowed down, moving with cautious alertness, ears sensitive to any alien sound. For a time he heard nothing but the raucous chattering of pericos and guacamayo birds.

Then, faint and barely distinguishable, he heard the sound of voices in the distance. He froze motionless, intently studying the immediate surroundings. Here the land had been untended for years; the young mahogany trees were choked with a mass of stunted bamboo and plantain trees and saw-toothed jungle grasses. Some fifteen feet to the left of the trail he spotted an ahuehuete tree that had grown at a sharp angle. Silently he moved towards it, then stood and considered the distance up to the first thick branches. He took off his shoes, knotted the laces together, hung them about his neck. Now his feet could get a better grip on the gnarled trunk. Cautiously he began the ascent.

He had to climb nearly to the top of the tree before he could peer through the thick foliage down into the hollow where the old mill stood. There was a clearing in front of the mill, to one side of the narrow stream. In the clearing a dozen men were lounging about. A few wore side arms, the others were unarmed.

So far none of them were in uniform.

Exactly who were they, he wondered. Some were doubtlessly remnants of the old Caribbean Legion, hiring out to the highest bidder. Others would be soldiers of fortune, drifters, misfits. Some few would be the inevitable idealists, certain that any change would be for the better.

It made no difference, he told himself. For whatever reason they had made their choice. Now they would have to pay the price.

He eased down the trunk of the ahuehuete, put his shoes back on. There was another entrance to the old mill, he remembered, a wide, window-like opening where the shaft of the water wheel entered. He doubted that it had ever been closed up. To reach it he would have to cross the stream, dangerously close to the clearing. And there was no certainty that there were not men lounging or sleeping inside the mill.

A diversion was needed.

Gould concentrated, dismissing one scheme after another that came to mind. Then he began circling through the thick underbrush until he was a dozen yards to one side of the trail, at a point on the opposite side of the mill from the stream. On the way his eyes searched the ground for dry twigs and branches, which he gathered up. Finally he reached a spot that seemed suited for his purpose. He dug out a shallow hollow in the spongy earth, carefully broke up some of the smallest twigs. He took out his lighter, flicked it into flame, and started a tiny fire. Slowly he fed it with slightly larger bits of wood until at the end of five minutes he had a small heap of hotly glowing coals.

He took a dozen cartridges out of one of the gun belts he had taken from the dwarf, dropped them into the center of the coals. On top he put more dry wood, bigger pieces this time.

Then he turned and made his way quickly back across the trail, moving as far as he dared towards the edge of the clearing.

He waited.

It was another two minutes before the first cartridge exploded. Then four others went off in quick succession. Sudden shouts came from the clearing. Flat on his stomach, Gould moved closer. He reached a vantage point where he could look down at the front of the mill. The men there were moving about uncertainly, staring in the direction of the shots. An older man, apparently the leader of the group, barked an order. The men, armed now with rifles that had been quickly distributed, spread out from the clearing, seeking cover in the surrounding bush.

Three more of the cartridges Gould had dumped in the fire exploded.

Rapidly, keeping hunched down, Gould began to circle the open space. He reached the narrow stream, plunged across, almost losing his footing on the slippery rocks. He scrambled up the opposite bank, shot a quick glance over his shoulder to see if he had been spotted, then headed upstream toward the water wheel.

Now the crumbling walls of the mill gave him protection. The wooden paddles of the water wheel had long since rotted away but the shaft, bound with bands of wrought iron, still stuck out from a wide opening high up in the wall. Gould studied the distance, then moved a few yards up the bank. He took a quick running jump, arms stretched upwards. His hands wrapped over the top of the shaft, fingers digging into the termite-porous wood.

For seconds he hung there, wondering how firm his purchase was. Gradually he tensed his arm muscles, drawing himself slowly up until he could fling one arm over the shaft. Then he was astride, inching towards the wall opening.

At first he could distinguish nothing in the deep shadows inside the mill. Then shadows took shape, became piled up crates and boxes.

Gould took a deep breath, edged cautiously through the opening. Just as he was about to drop to the ground a sound caught his attention. Turning his head he saw a man carrying a rifle moving into the open doorway, his figure silhouetted against the bright sunlight.

It took a fraction of a second for Gould to make up his mind, less time than it took to draw one of the .45's and fire. He saw the man stagger and fall. He gambled that those outside would think the shot came from the woods where the last of the cartridges were now exploding.

He hesitated another moment, then dropped to the ground inside the mill. His eyes were now accustomed to the semi-obscurity. Hurriedly he scanned the piled up boxes. There were crates of rifles, Thompson machine guns, ammunition. All regular U. S. Army issue.

At last he found what he had been praying would be there, a heavy crate of hand grenades. He hunted around, found a broken machete, used it to pry the crate open. Taking out half a dozen of the grenades he hung them on his holster belt. Then he upended one of the boxes, mounted it and swung back up into the wall opening.

Once outside he dropped to the ground. Pulling the pin on one of the grenades he hurled it over the mill in the direction of the clearing. He followed it quickly with a second. That should be enough to send the motley band of would-be insurrectionists deeper into the bush.

In swift succession he lobbed three grenades through the shaft opening into the mill. The explosions of the second and third merged with a heavier detonation as the boxes of ammunition went off. Then the crate of grenades exploded. As he scrambled across the rocky bed of the stream Gould glanced over his shoulder. He saw the tiled roof of the old mill belly upwards, as though the whole structure had drawn a deep and final breath. Then it disappeared in the grating sound of crumbling rubble.

Gould regarded the scene of destruction for a speculative moment of grim satisfaction before striking off again through the woods. He was uncertain as to the exact distance to Norden's hacienda but figured it could be no more than ten kilometers at the most. His own property ended less than a kilometer beyond the mill stream; another twelve kilometers and the mountain range that blocked off Lago Cristobal from the sea rose abruptly.

The German's main house had to be somewhere between, in all probability bordering the lake. Further, he had a strong hunch that by now there must be a fairly well-traveled trail leading from the old mill to Norden's place.

A few minutes later he found it.

For a time he moved swiftly along, putting as much distance behind him as possible. Then instinctive caution asserted itself. He stepped off the trail and into the thick, concealing brush that bordered the path. With the added need of quiet the going was much slower. In the end the precaution might prove needless, Gould told himself, but the habit was ingrained. At short intervals he paused for a space of several minutes to listen intently.

It was a half an hour later that he heard the sound. Muffled voices suddenly broken off as though by some impatient command. Gould sprawled face down in the thick underbrush, moving slightly so that he could look back along the trail. His right hand gripped one of the .45's. It was a weapon he had never liked, never trusted. He hoped the damned thing wouldn't jam when most needed, as sometimes happened.

A moment later he saw the figures advancing. The flat-faced Indian who had stood guard the night before in the dining room was in the lead, followed closely by two younger men in soiled pants and once white shirts who gave the unmistakable appearance of being city-bred. All three were armed, the Indian still carrying the Garand.

Briefly Gould wondered if they were on their way to warn Norden of what had happened, or on his track, or both. One way or another it didn't matter.

He waited until the group was less than a dozen yards away. He raised the .45 slightly. As he did so a dry branch snapped under him and the Indian in a sudden swift movement swung his rifle in the direction of the sound.

Gould fired twice, one slug shattering the Indian's right arm, the other hammering with deadly precision through his heart.

He turned his attention to the two younger men who were standing now in shocked fright, uncertain of their next move. Gould turned the .45 on them but at the last moment, prompted by a compassion for fools, deflected his aim slightly. He drilled both through the right shoulder, watched with a bitter smile as they dropped their guns and ran keening with pain back down the trail.

He waited a moment, still listening intently, before he straightened up and moved forward. He picked up the Garand, prodded the lifeless body of the Indian with his foot, then turned and started on.

Glancing at his watch he saw it was exactly two-thirty.

CHAPTER SEVENTEEN

IT WAS shortly after four when a turn in the trail brought Gould to a quick stop. Ahead the forest thinned out abruptly, the underbrush was neatly cleaned and pruned. Through the trees he could see the grounds that surrounded Norden's place, well-tended lawns and gardens that swept down to the edge of the lake.

The main house, Gould noted, was comparatively new—built in the abortive Spanish colonial style that he had always considered one of the less attractive features of Southern California. There were a number of smaller outlying buildings. As Gould skirted through the trees he saw that outside one of the larger buildings a small helicopter was stationed. He saw no workmen or mechanics about. There was a new Chevrolet sedan that seemed vaguely familiar parked at one end of the curving driveway.

Thoughtfully he studied the main building, a long, narrow structure. Although from his angle it was not visible he had a strong hunch that the living room would have a picture window facing the lake. Such houses always did.

Still keeping under the cover of the woods Gould made a semi-circuit around the back of the house. On the side of the main entrance he saw the dusty black Daimler. Close by was the figure of a squat Indian holding a rifle negligently in the crook of an arm, standing lazily on guard as he stared out over the lake.

Gould doubled back on his tracks until an ell of the building blocked him from the Indian's sight. Drawing a deep breath he mentally crossed his fingers and then walked boldly out of the sheltering woods.

As he neared the side of the house he held the Garand in easy firing position, praying that he wouldn't be forced to use it too soon. He rounded the corner of the ell. The Indian still had his back turned, gazing out over the water.

Gould moved swiftly, hunched down to keep below the windows in the rear of the house. At the last minute he reversed the Garand, holding it by the barrel. He swung with bone-crushing force against the side of the Indian's neck, heard something crack as the man dropped.

Stepping over the lifeless body Gould peered around the corner of the building. No one was in sight. It was three more steps to the front door. Gently he twisted the heavy brass knob, gave an inward sigh of satisfaction when the latch turned and the door swung open.

Standing in the cool, shadowy entrance hall he heard the sound of voices in an adjoining room.

He moved forward a step and was able to identify the speakers. One was unmistakably Norden; the other, lower and less sharply pronounced, was the voice of a woman.

Gould pushed through a half open door into the living room.

Norden, comfortably seated in a wicker lounge chair, was saying impatiently, "I tell you again, I know what I am doing. It would have been stupid to kill him outright, without apparent cause. As it is—" He broke off suddenly at the sound of the closing door. Any expression in his eyes was masked by the dark glasses. But Gould saw his fingers tighten on the chair arms until the knuckles gleamed whitely.

The woman had been standing with her back to the room, staring out of the picture window. Now she swirled about. It was, as Gould suspected, Clare Hammet.

For a speechless moment she stared at him as though she were seeing a ghost. Then she flared out at Norden, "I told you so! You wouldn't listen …"

Without turning his head in her direction the German raised a hand. "Quiet!"

Gould leaned his back against the door. "Don't let me interrupt you. I believe you were discussing when and how I should be put out of the way."

"A matter still open for discussion," Norden suggested coldly.

"Quite possibly." Gould smiled at him thinly. "But for you the subject is closed. Finished. Along with your neat little plans for sabotaging the United States."

"You lie! I have too many men for you to stop me."

"Not now you haven't. Your charming dwarf Pepe met with a slight accident. So did your pistolero, Mario. Both are dead."

"Animals! They are not important."

Again Gould permitted himself the self-indulgence of a faint smile. He said casually, "And your caché of arms in the old mill? Is that, too, no longer of importance?"

"It is well guarded."

"Not now. It no longer exists. I am surprised you didn't hear the sound of the explosion even at this distance."

Norden sat silently, his pale, bloodless lips set in a straight line. Clare Hammet cried out, "I warned you. We should not have wasted time trying to frighten him out of San Barrios. We should have handled him as we did Hobart Drake."

Norden said sharply, "We weren't certain at the beginning that he was actually a Washington agent. Even your husband didn't suspect."

"I did! I felt it from the start. A woman knows certain things intuitively."

Gould decided he had heard enough. He said, "Suppose you save your recriminations for another time and place. The local juzgado, perhaps. The game is up. Finished."

"No." Norden spoke up with a new assurance in his voice. "It is not finished."

Gould studied him thoughtfully through narrowed eyes. "And why not?"

"Because an intelligent leader always plans for the unforeseen." The German's voice became pedantically precise. "I am going to escape, my friend, and you are going to allow me to leave. But not alone. The lady goes with me. And afterwards you will say nothing about what has taken place."

"An interesting suggestion," Gould said lazily. "Just why will this happen?"

"Because I presume you still have the interests of your country at heart. True, you could shoot me down now but that would leave the problem of what to do with Frau Hammet. Supposing you are callous enough to murder her in cold blood. How would you explain it? Could you say that the wife of your ambassador to this country was a traitor? That would be embarrassing. Who would believe you? What solid proof could you offer? You see my point?"

"Well thought out," Gould admitted grimly. "But why should my lips remain sealed after you have made this neatly planned escape?"

"For much the same reasons. The lady goes with me. That can always be explained as an affair of the heart. In reality she will be my insurance for your silence. If you attempt to expose me she will immediately start giving interviews to the newspapers in that particular South American country where I also have a secret base of operations. She will say she left her husband because she learned of the imperialistic plans of your country to further subjugate the Latin American peoples by military intervention. It is a story that will be readily believed by both the leftists and nationalists in every country south of the border. All the denials in the world won't wipe out the suspicion that possibly the story is true."

Gould nodded, said evenly, "It looks like check-mate, doesn't it?"

"Exactly." The German stood up slowly. Gould shifted the Garand, keeping it trained in readiness. Norden said, "Come here, Clare."

When she stood beside him the tall, beautifully developed figure of the American Ambassador's wife dwarfed the slight build of the German. In the back of his mind Bart Gould gave a faint sigh, thinking of how that lush, sex-conscious beauty was being wasted.

Norden was speaking again. "We are walking out of the door now, señor Gould, and down to the helicopter you can see through the window. I keep it always in readiness for just such an emergency as this. I, myself, am an expert pilot. But it is only fair to warn you that I shall not forget what you have done. We will meet again some day to settle accounts."

"It will be a pleasure." Gould told him, his tone expressionless. "Now why don't you get on your way."

He followed them out of the door. His slate-grey eyes cold and remorseless he watched as they crossed the green sweep of lawn with its spongy Bermuda grass towards the helicopter. They climbed in, and in the still quiet of the late afternoon he heard the electric starter, saw the overhead propellors start lazily turning.

Norden had been right, he thought wearily. How did you tell an ambassador, dedicated to his work and his country, that his wife was a traitor? How did you explain such things so as to hurt the fewest people possible?

There was no answer. Or rather, there was only one.

He watched the helicopter begin to rise slowly and then move out over the lake.

It was a hundred yards distant—a hundred and fifty—then two hundred yards.

The lines on Bart Gould's lean hawk-face tightened, grew hard. He raised the Garand, sighted, began firing, aiming towards the high-test gas tanks.

For a moment he thought he had waited too long. Then the stream of bullets found its mark. There was a sudden burst of flame—for brief seconds the helicopter was a motionless ball of fire in the sky before it plunged downward, disappeared in a final explosive burst in the blue-black waters.

Poetic justice, he tried to tell himself. Now the score has been evened, Hobart Drake. If it makes any difference …

In the distance he heard the sound of a car approaching at top speed.

CHAPTER EIGHTEEN

BART GOULD stepped quickly back into the house, standing just inside the open doorway where he could watch the final stretch of the private road that led from the distant highway.

A moment later he saw the car, a dirt-grey sedan. It roared off the dirt road onto the driveway, then skidded to a rubber-scorching stop as the driver jammed on his brakes. From the back of the car three soldiers carrying light machine guns stepped out and stood looking suspiciously around.

From the front of the car an older man, also in uniform, emerged. As he walked towards the house Gould recognized him as Colonel Rodríguez. He waited until the army officer was a dozen paces away. Then he leaned the Garand out of sight against the hallway wall and stepped through the open doorway.

"Buenos tardes, coronel."

Rodríguez stopped short, eyeing him intently for a long moment before he spoke in a tone of exasperation mingled with relief. "It is indeed my lucky day. You give me much worry, señor Gould. I did not expect to find you alive."

Gould's nerves tensed with sudden suspicion. "For what reason?"

Rodríguez shrugged, took out a sheer linen handkerchief and mopped his face. "I received a warning—a most curious and involved story—from a young woman of dubious standing. It appears you have a way with the ladies, señor." He paused, waited, and when Gould made no comment went on, "She was certain that you would be found here or at your own place and that the possibilities were most strong that you would be found dead if we did not arrive in time. When I heard the sound of shooting and saw a plane go down in flames just a moment ago I was sure that it was too late."

"It was not a plane," Gould corrected. "It was a helicopter. One in which Herr Norden was attempting to kidnap señora Hammet, the wife of my country's ambassador here. The machine apparently exploded. Probably a leaky fuel line or something of the sort."

"And the shots?"

Gould gave the answer without hesitation. "Norden was firing at me. I had discovered too much of certain of his plans against your government and he wanted me out of the way." Leaning against the wall, Gould pulled out cigarettes. He held out the package to the colonel who shook his head, then lit one for himself. "It is fortunate that you arrived when you did, colonel. There is a nasty little mess around here to be cleaned up. Norden had arranged for an armed uprising, scheduled to take place in a day or so. Apparently at the last moment something went wrong and he must have lost control of the mob he had recruited. There are always casualties when such affairs are badly planned, no?"

A frown creasing his sweat-beaded forehead the colonel said doubtfully, "You are quite certain? I have heard various rumors, but they did not Involve the señor Norden."

"You can see the evidence for yourself. He even made use of the old mill on the edge of my property to store his arms. Probably efforts have been made to destroy that evidence by now, but if you are in time you may be able to round up the remnants of his little private army." Gould paused, regarded the tip of his cigarette for a thoughtful moment, then looked calmly back at

Rodríguez. "I'm sure your *presidente* will appreciate it if the matter is handled quietly and without fuss. With so many delegates for the O.A.S. conference in the country the wrong kind of publicity could prove highly embarrassing."

Rodríguez sighed heavily and gave his head a slight shake. "Ay, hombre! And to think that my orders were to see that no harm came to you."

Gould laughed and clapped him on the shoulder. "I shall inform the *presidente* that you have done your work well. Now I must get back to my hacienda and pick up the car de la Vega loaned me. It is one of his favorites and he is probably worrying about it even now." Then, walking with the colonel towards the army car, he dropped a deliberate teaser. "I have an idea that shortly I will be looking for a new estate manager. It is possible that you might help me find the right man."

Rodríguez silently digested the suggestion. Finally he reached out and opened the car door, waving Gould into the front seat beside the driver.

"Si, señor Gould," he said. "It is more than possible."

At night there was little traffic over the mountain road. Gould concentrated on the road and speed, trying to dismiss from his mind the events of the past twenty-four hours, trying not to think of the immediate future and the manner in which the news would have to be broken to Roger Hammet that his wife had been the victim of a tragic accident.

So much would have to be left unsaid, so much left unexplained. It would be better that way.

It was a little after eleven when he parked the Cord on the side street by the Palace Hotel. Wearily he stretched his aching muscles. He walked through the cantina, crowded at this hour with delegates to the O.A.S. conference heatedly debating the latest twist in Argentine politics. Gould was tempted to stop for a moment and then decided against it. What he wanted now most of all was solitude and rest. A drink, a hot bath, another drink and then food and bed.

He stopped at the desk for his key. There were a number of messages in his box which he shoved in his pocket without reading. They could wait until tomorrow.

He walked up the curving marble stairs to the second floor and down the wide corridor to his room. When he inserted the key and turned it he discovered that the door was unlocked.

Now what? he wondered wearily. He stepped far to one side, reached out and turned the knob. With a sudden thrust he sent the door wide open.

For a moment nothing happened. Then a softly feminine voice demanded nervously, "Quien es?"

Once again Bart Gould had an unannounced visitor waiting for him.

As he stepped into the room Paquita jumped up from the chair in which she had been sitting stiffly upright. "You are back! Then they didn't find you?"

Gould eyed her with curious speculation as he crossed to the table, picked up the rum bottle and poured himself a sizable drink. He took a long sip before answering, watching the singer over the rim of his glass. "I don't know whether they found me or not," he said finally. "But you can see for yourself that I am back."

"I wanted to warn you only you wouldn't stop long enough to listen!"

"Oh?" Gould took another sip of rum, felt the soothing warmth of it spread slowly through his tired body. He continued studying the girl with half-closed eyes. She was wearing a dress of dark magenta jersey silk, cut so as to emphasize her narrow waist, full breasts and the outward curve of her hips. When she moved the material clung with revealing intimacy to her thighs. "And just why did you want to warn me?. "

She made an impatient gesture. "Because I became involved in something I didn't understand. I wished to correct my mistake before it was too late." She waited, and when Gould continued watching her in quizzical silence, burst out, "You do not believe me, but it is true! When you wouldn't stop to listen to me I went to see your friend, the newspaper editor. I told him they were waiting for you at your hacienda to kill you. He went with me to a coronel Rodríguez to repeat the story. And then I came here to wait. The coronel promised to advise me if you were safe but he did not do so."

"I imagine he has been otherwise occupied." Gould lifted his glass, saw that it was empty and reached for the rum bottle. He started to pour, then looked at the girl. "Would you like a drink?"

"A very small one, please."

"Right. Now suppose you tell me what your boy friend Ramón has been doing all this time."

With the fingertips of one hand she made an erasing movement in the air. "He has gone. When he learned that I was going to the authorities he called me many bad names and tried to stop me. But he is a coward. I think that by now he is across the border on his way to Cuba."

"A dubious gain for Castro." Taking another swallow of rum, regarding the girl with automatically appreciative eyes, Gould remarked to himself on the curious fact that he no longer felt so wearily tired as he had a short time before. He said, "How is it that you are not at the Flamingo tonight?"

She shrugged. "I do not think I have work there any more. The manager is muy enojado comigo. Very angry."

"I imagine that can be smoothed over. I'll have de la Vega speak to the manager."

"Thank you, señor." She stood there, fingering the glass in her hand, making no move to leave.

Gould said casually, "Is there anything else on your mind?"

She gave him a veiled look. "I was about to ask you the same thing, señor."

"Easily answered. I plan to take a hot and cold shower, have some food, and then go to bed."

"I could wait while you take your shower," Paquita suggested softly. "It is not always pleasant to eat alone."

"A nice thought." Gould started for the bedroom and then had a sudden thought. He turned back. "Suppose while I'm in the shower you telephone the Flamingo and reserve a table. You might also order *pavita parrillada* so that it will be ready when we get there. I was unable to enjoy it the other night because a girl I was anxious to talk to ran out on me."

Reaching for the telephone Paquita gave him a long look over her shoulder. "I promise you, señor, that tonight I will not run …"

CHAPTER NINETEEN

IT WAS exactly six o'clock in the evening.

Bart Gould had been back in Washington for a little over an hour. He had stayed on in San Barrios long enough to see the O.A.S. conference get under way without incident and to hear Roger Hammet, bearing up remarkably well under his bereavement, give the opening address to the delegates.

Now he sat in his study, relaxing over a drink, considering the pleasantly empty hours ahead.

The telephone rang.

From the master phone below, Hobbs said, "Mr. Banning on the wire, sir."

Gould sighed. He had deliberately refrained from advising the mystery man of the White House of his return, wanting time to decide just how much to tell. Or, more to the point, what not to tell.

A moment later, the connection made, the dry New England voice said tersely, "Glad to learn you're back. A car will pick you up in twenty minutes."

A wave of stubbornness made Gould protest. "Suppose I happen to have a prior engagement?"

"Break it!"

Gould sighed again and hung up.

Forty-five minutes later he was once again sitting uncomfortably in the austere, bleakly furnished White House office of Titus Banning.

He waited, refusing to break the silence with which he had been greeted.

Finally Banning spoke. "Gather your trip was successful?"

Gould answered that one with a question that was more of a statement. "You've had no more anonymous threats, have you?"

"Nope." Banning bit off the word sharply. "Don't want to know the details. Less a man knows, sometimes, less he has to fret about. Only one thing troubles me a mite."

Gould waited.

"Hammet's wife. Was she mixed up in the mess?"

Gould said carefully, "Let us just say that she happened to be in the wrong place at the wrong time. A regrettable but under the circumstances—" he hesitated, looking for the right word, "—unavoidable accident."

Banning's frosty eyes studied him intently. Then he half grunted, "I see. In your judgment it couldn't be helped."

"No."

The New Englander nodded briefly, as though dismissing the subject once and for all. His thin lips twitched slightly as he said, "Had a report on you."

Gould felt himself tense angrily. His slate-grey eyes narrowed as he leaned forward. "I thought—"

Banning stopped him with an upraised hand. "Unsolicited. Didn't ask for it. Wish some of the busy-body snooping agencies would stick to their own knitting." He fingered some papers on his desk, selected one. "According to this report, you spent most of your time in San Barrios carousing in public places with a nightclub singer. Projecting a very bad image of an American citizen at a crucial time when the country was full of important delegates to the O.A.S. conference. A suggestion was made to Ambassador Hammet that he speak to you but, to quote, he indignantly refused."

For the first time since coming into the office Gould laughed. "Sounds like one of J. Edgar's boys."

Banning said sharply, "You know as well as I do that they are not authorized to work outside the country."

"I know." Gould returned his frosty stare with one of bland innocence. "Amazing, isn't it, how over-staffed the commercial attaché's offices are with anonymous young men in such places as San Barrios?"

Banning snorted, then again changed the subject abruptly. "Know anything about Vienna?"

Gould paused in the act of lighting one of his Havana cigarettes. He said warily, "Just as a casual tourist. Very little, really."

Banning looked at him steadily for a moment before reaching into a desk drawer and drawing out a folder. He flicked through it as though to refresh his memory. In his dry New England twang he said, "Four years ago you had a six months' lease on an apartment on the Rennweg. You also had a hunting lodge in the Austrian Tyrol for the same length of time. There was also a Baroness Mitzi Uexcuell, a widow, age thirty-five at the time—"

"Twenty-eight," Gould broke in, his thoughts suddenly nostalgic. "That was all she admitted to and she looked less than that."

Banning's lips set in prim disapproval. "Be that as it may. Point is, you know Vienna. More than a little bit, from the looks of the record. It may be that we have a problem coming up there."

Gould stood up quickly. "Fine. And you can get somebody else to handle it. Now if you don't mind I'll be on my way."

Banning stopped him. "One more thing. I was instructed to advise you that you have an engagement to play tennis at precisely eleven-fifteen tomorrow. I was further instructed to warn you, and I quote, to be on your toes or you'd get your—ah—pants run ragged."

For the second time during the brief interview Bart Gould laughed. "I'll lay you ten to one, money or marbles, that he didn't say 'pants'."

www.ingramcontent.com/pod-product-compliance
Lightning Source LLC
Chambersburg PA
CBHW052010240626
47153CB00008B/2813

9781970848021